FOURTEEN FOR TONIGHT

FOURTEEN FOR TONIGHT

by
STEVE ALLEN

HENRY HOLT AND COMPANY
New York

To

MY MOTHER

CONTENTS

FOURTEEN
FOR
TONIGHT

1

THE SOUTHERN ACCENT

My father died when I was a baby and from then on in I was raised by women, but there was one man I remember being around the house pretty often. Uncle Jack. Oh, I had a stepfather for a while, but he faded out of the picture before I was six years old and I don't remember him very clearly. And there was Uncle Bill, but he usually worked in some other city like Allentown, Pennsylvania, or Los Angeles. He only came home to Chicago to visit and then, at the end, to die.

But Jack was around quite a lot. He would go away for five or six months at a time, usually to a soldiers' home. Sometimes he would go to the one in Danville, Illinois, and sometimes to one in Wisconsin; I think it was at West Allis. Sometimes, too, he would just go away, period, and neither my mother nor any of her sisters would have the slightest idea where he had gone.

"I'm worried sick," my mother would say. "We haven't heard from Jack in eight weeks."

"Oh, don't worry, Bella," her sister Kate would say; "he'll turn up. If anything had happened to him you'd have heard about it."

Kate was just as worried as Mother, but they'd take turns cheering each other up. Both of them were confirmed pessimists but never at the same time. Whichever one picked up the pessimism first sort of had a claim on it. The other would automatically assume the role of the optimist, although always with a certain lack of conviction.

Sure enough, Jack would turn up eventually or else they'd get a brief letter from him. It was always just one page long and it always began "Dear Sister." It was neither an overly friendly letter nor a cold one, but the fact that he had cared enough to write made the letter a gladsome thing to the women. The handwriting was always neat and all the words were spelled correctly, although the punctuation and the grammar left something to be desired. No one in my mother's family had ever got beyond a fifth-grade education.

The letters usually went something like this:

Just thought I would drop you a line to tell you that I have been here at Danville for the past couple of months. I have gained twelve pounds and am eating like an army mule. The weather here is good and I am

off the drink and feeling fine. I hope you are all well.
Take care of yourselves.

Your loving brother.

I never did know why Jack kept going away and coming back, although his departures usually followed a siege of heavy drinking and a big fight. He would be on the straight and narrow for several weeks, and then all of a sudden one day he wouldn't show up at all for maybe two days. When he would come home he'd be drunk and ugly and mean and he'd insult my mother and all her sisters and swear and throw up in the bathroom. And his clothes would be dirty, as if he had slept on the sidewalk or in some alley.

He'd rant and rave around the house for maybe twenty-four hours and he'd smash drinking glasses and threaten to kill Kate and my mother, but he never laid a hand on them and through it all he was never angry or cross with me. That part was funny. Uncle Bill was actually a better human being than Jack, I suppose; he was intelligent, usually had a good job, was a neat dresser, and had a lot of friends. But he was always very strict with me. So for that one crazy reason I preferred Jack.

When he was sober and in good spirits Uncle Jack would take me to Lincoln Park Zoo or to the circus or just for long walks in the park. At every street we crossed he'd lecture me about looking both ways for traffic; and as we walked along in the morning air he'd tell me to take deep breaths and to keep my back straight like a soldier. I had been sickly as a young child and, having spent such a lot of time in bed being pampered and fussed over, I suppose I had gotten a little delicate in personality as well as in body. I think this worried Jack because he was always telling me about people like Teddy Roosevelt and Jack Dempsey, and he was always telling me to throw back my shoulders and to breathe deeply and to drink lots of milk and to get lots of exercise.

Like a lot of the Irish who grew up back of the Yards, he had never had an opportunity to be trained in any particular trade. That's not a real excuse for not making anything of yourself, of course, but it has something to do with it. Jack's own father was a strict, violent-tempered immigrant who married a docile, saintly girl and had sixteen children by her. Most of them died either at birth or shortly after, but those who grew up were rebellious and wild, all of them. Frankly, there wasn't one person in my mother's family who had what you and I would call good sense. They had a lot of other abilities: they were bright, amusing, popular, charitable, honest to an uncommon degree, religious in their own peculiar way, and, except for Jack, hard-working. But they were all wild and unpredictable and terrible-tempered like their father. The father was so hard and the mother so soft that the children's personalities got twisted out of shape. They never learned tolerance or logic or intellectual curiosity or a love for the arts. They lived at either the father's or the mother's emotional extreme. They were either loving each other furiously or hating each other with an equal fury. The hatred never lasted, of course, but it was in the saddle just long enough to break up home after home. I can remember living in at least a dozen different places when I was a child, and in each case the reason for moving was that there had been a fight and somebody had said, "I can't stand this. I've got to get out of this neighborhood and find some peace."

So Jack had the least sense of all, but I liked him. He used to feel the muscle on my scrawny upper arm and pretend to marvel at its firmness. And no matter how drunk he got, no matter how angry his hidden resentments made him at the rest of the world, he could always, even in the midst of his violent rages, be gentle with me. And he had reason, sometimes, to be angry with me too. I remember one time when we lived on Cottage Grove Avenue our apartment had a long, narrow, dark hallway that ran from the living room, past a bedroom and a bathroom, back to the dining room. I used to be afraid of the dark, I think, and I never liked to walk through this hallway. One day when I was hurrying along its dismal length, Uncle Jack made a sudden noise behind a drapery and said, "Boo!" Although he meant to frighten me he was just playing, but I didn't understand that at the time. I was in the instant overcome by fear and shock and in my sudden rage I kicked at him as hard as I could. I was only about seven, but I had on new shoes and in my anger I must have put great force into the kick. I remember the point of the new shoe caught his leg squarely on the shinbone and he exhaled slightly as he felt the pain. But he didn't get angry at me. He just held me at arm's length for a moment till I calmed down and then he laughed a little and apologized. He carried the scar on his shin for many months.

That must have been one of the times when he would go off and sit by himself somewhere in the house and read and whistle. When his mind was on something else he either whistled or softly sang an old song called "Sunbonnet Sue."

"Sunbonnet Sue . . . Sunbonnet Sue," he would whisper softly, "sunshine and roses run second to you. I kissed you twice . . . it was so nice . . . under your bonnet of blue."

So far as I was ever able to learn, the singing of this lyric was Uncle Jack's one concession to the fact that love and/or sex existed in the world. He never married and he never spoke of women except, as I say, when he sang, "It was only a kind of a kid-kiss, but it tasted much nicer than pie. What else could I do? I was dead stuck on you . . . when you were a kid so high." I don't even know if those were the right words, but that's the way he used to sing it.

Jack was what you would call a confirmed bachelor, but not of the usual type, if there is a usual type. By that I mean he was not an artistic homosexual, nor was he the Caspar Milquetoast mama's boy. Physically he was big, manly. He looked like a stevedore or a truck driver. He always wore secondhand dark blue suits and a rough-looking gray cap. Except on rare occasions he would not wear a tie, and his shirts were the sort worn by railroad men. He drank hard and got into fist fights at the drop of a hat. When he was young I presume he fought because he was almost certain to win; but as he got older he used to come home obviously the loser of these saloon altercations, his shirt sometimes encrusted with blood and his face and lips cut and swollen. He didn't have enough sense to stop picking fights with other, younger men.

No, Jack was a bachelor of a type that I think might possibly be peculiar to the Irish. I seem to recall reading an article a couple of years ago in some magazine that said that the birth rate in Ireland is falling at an alarming rate and that there are far too many bachelors and old maids over there. Nobody has as yet pinned down the precise reasons, but there are a lot of theories. Some blame the Church, but there are many Catholic countries and only Ireland has this peculiar problem. Some blame the climate, others the poverty of the farmers, others the puritanical traditions of the country. Whatever the reason, it produces a certain number of men like Jack: virile, fearless, completely masculine, but shy with women to an unnatural degree, unsophisticated, narrow-minded, old-fashioned, out of contact with their time, almost monastically sexless.

If there was any explanation of Jack's inability to hold a job, it might be the one sometimes put forth by my mother: that as the baby of the family he was the most protected by his mother. But these days it is the fashion to say that it is the oldest child in the family who usually has the roughest road and that the baby, because he gets more love and attention, has more confidence in himself and his world.

I'm no psychiatrist and I can't figure it out any more than the rest of the family could. You can point to social environment and you've got a pretty fair argument, because the South Side of Chicago in the early years of the century was a rough, brawling place to grow up in, with plenty of saloons and pool halls but no playgrounds or libraries or young people's dances. But then again, millions of other people grew up in that same environment and they didn't all turn out to be hard-drinking saloon fighters.

When I got a little older I sometimes used to envy men like Jack their lack of interest in sex. And I suppose men like Jack envy me my lack of interest in liquor. I've been lucky, of course, in that you can channel your sexual appetite correctly, but there's no earthly good can come of a lusty appetite for alcohol.

But maybe I'm getting off the track. Another reason I liked Jack was that he had a great sense of humor. He never told jokes or stories and he wasn't the life of the party type by a long shot; but in ordinary conversation he could perceive and isolate the humorous element. Too, he had a few little meaningless phrases he used to say to me that always amused me although I never really understood them.

"Do you know Tap Max?" he used to say to me when he was just slightly drunk.

"Who's that?" I would demand, in mock seriousness because I knew he was playing with me.

"He's a friend of Calingo Red's," Jack would say.

"Who's Calingo Red?"

"He works with Tap Max."

Once in a while Jack would say something about Tap Max or Calingo Red being in the Rocky Mountains working on some railroad or other, but I never found out who they were. Jack used to talk a lot about railroads. He worked for different lines, and of course when he traveled it was always on freights. I think he always fancied himself a railroad man, although he had probably not worked long at any particular railroad jobs either. He used to dress like railroad men and roll his own cigarettes with Bull Durham tobacco (I used to save the little cloth bags to keep marbles in), and in his back pocket he always carried a large dark blue handkerchief with white dots.

I liked him, too, because he was a solid masculine influence in the sometimes cloyingly feminine world in which I lived as a child. My aunt used to praise him sometimes when he was away. "He was a handsome man when he was younger," she would say. "He looked like Gary Cooper." I never thought Jack looked like Gary Cooper but he had the same tall, lean open-airness about him. He used to talk not only of railroads but of the Far West and of farms and mountains and army life and the oil fields. He had traveled a lot. The one place I do not believe he ever visited was the South. And that was peculiar because when he got drunk he would speak with a Southern accent.

Not when he was angry, of course; just when he was trying to be amusing.

I remember one night when we lived on 60th Street just off Halsted and he came home drunk and wild. He broke some dishes in the kitchen and chased Kate to bed and told my mother to go to hell, so the three of us went to bed and left him roaming around the house, cursing and mumbling to himself and bumping into things.

I slept with my aunt in the front bedroom. There was a very small porch just off this bedroom which could be entered from the living room. After I lay in the darkness whispering to my aunt for perhaps half an hour a storm began to come up. I remember watching the lights of cars making patterns on the ceiling and walls of the room as they drove past in the rain.

It was then we heard the door to the porch open.

"He's going out there in the rain," my aunt hissed.

Sure enough, Jack walked out on the small porch, muttering to himself; I saw him clearly as a flash of lightning washed the scene white. And then I laughed because he had come home with a peculiar haircut, with the hair much too short and looking almost like a convict's, and he was standing out on the porch in his long underwear.

There was an old-fashioned deck chair on the porch and I knew if he tried to sit in it he would have trouble; I was not surprised when suddenly I heard the sound of the chair being knocked and pulled about and Jack swearing.

"Is he going to sleep out there in the rain?" I asked my aunt, giggling at the prospect.

"Shut up," she whispered. "If he hears you laughing

he'll keep that foolishness up all night, if it doesn't make him mad."

The wind was stronger now and I heard Jack say in a loud voice, "Blow, you son-of-a-bitch, blow!" The wind obliged and he must have been drenched to the skin. I seem to recall that he had been having trouble with his false teeth and that he was not wearing them that night. He must have presented a fearsome appearance. "My God," my aunt said, "if anybody sees him out there like that we'll all be arrested."

At this moment the wind died down a bit, and as the rain was not falling heavily I was able to hear the click-click of a man's heels coming down the sidewalk that ran right below the porch. When my aunt heard the foot-steps she said, "Jesus, Mary, and Joseph."

Then in the momentary stillness, over the soft sighing of the wind, as the heel sounds passed just below our window I heard Jack say, "Say, brothah . . ."

From below there came a startled, "What!"

"Pahdon me, podnuh," said Jack, speaking with the mellow accents of the South, "but ah was wonderin' if pe'haps you maght have a cigarette."

I remember getting a fit of the giggles and laughing so hard my aunt had to press her hand over my mouth. I don't remember what happened after that. I must have fallen asleep happy.

2

THE PIGEON

Mrs. Patchford was passing Brooks Brothers when she saw the pigeon.

The day was gloriously autumnal, although on Madison Avenue Mrs. Patchford could only perceive the fact by reason of the briskness in the air. There were no trees visible and she was able to walk scuffingly through no fallen leaves, to tramp across no browned grass. There was just the sharp, winy bite in the air and the exhilarating chill of it against her ankles.

Overhead the sky, showing in regularly edged rectangles of pale blue, was bracing and footballish, but Mrs. Patchford did not lift her head to look at it. Instead she peered in an interested and intense manner into the face of each person who walked past her.

This was a custom of hers of which she was rather

proud. One day she had been walking past the Sherry-
Netherlands with Polly Gordon and she had suddenly
whirled and grasped Polly's arm and said, "There's
Harold Stassen!"

"Who?" said Polly. "Where?"

"Harold Stassen," Mrs. Patchford hissed. "There,
going into the hotel. Oh, you missed him!"

"Well," said Polly, "I guess I did, all right. That's
too bad."

"It's funny you didn't see him. He walked right past
us on your side. You practically touched him. Weren't
you looking at him?"

"No," Polly said. "I guess I'm not very observant
about things like that. I never notice anybody on the
street."

"I can't understand being like that," Mrs. Patchford
said disapprovingly. "*I* notice everything. I look at auto-
mobile licenses and children playing and people's faces
and everything. You miss a great deal when you don't
see what you're looking at."

Polly had admitted that she was probably right and
from that time on Mrs. Patchford, who until the Harold
Stassen incident had never really formulated her phi-
losophy of observant pedestrianism, became acutely
aware that she was possessed of an innate and long-
dormant gift worthy of further cultivation.

It was not an unusual thing therefore that of all the
people who had walked by the pigeon during the time
he had been standing in front of Brooks Brothers only

Mrs. Patchford brought the full power of her attention to bear upon him.

She was in a pleasant and expansive and slightly adventurous mood anyway. It was just a few minutes before eleven o'clock in the morning and she had just come from her doctor's office where the results of a series of tests of one kind and another had been made known to her.

"You're in great shape, Eleanor," Dr. Curtis had said. "Fit as a fiddle."

She had walked out of the office and started to hum something airy before she had even got off the elevator. The brown spot on her forearm had been worrying her for over three months, and then there had been the thing with the gall bladder. But now Curtis had wiped the slate clean and life was wonderful and she was eagerly looking forward to the stop at Bonwit's and then after that the visit to the hairdresser's. She would now, she considered, let Jeanette touch up the gray spots and try a deeper shade of red. When she thought of what Peter would say about her hair she giggled.

It was just at the moment she giggled that she saw the pigeon.

He was a small bird standing alone on a ledge about two feet above the sidewalk just to the right of Brooks Brothers door on the Madison Avenue side.

Unlike most of the pigeons of the St. Patrick's Cathedral covey he was not gray but tan, with streaks of white and deeper brown.

It was not the fact that he was huddled on the stone ledge that intrigued Mrs. Patchford, for the pigeons of Manhattan are an extraordinarily cool and reserved breed and they walk and fly among the bustling human and vehicular traffic with a great deal of aplomb. What made her stop in her tracks and look down at him was that he had not moved an inch as she brushed past him.

"Well," she said, "hello, there."

The bird regarded her calmly although he did not look at her eyes. He looked straight ahead so that he was looking at her knees.

"What's the matter?" she said, as if talking to a strange child.

The pigeon hobbled clumsily away from her and came to a halt after having traveled a distance of about eighteen inches along the ledge.

"Why, you poor little thing," Mrs. Patchford sang lovingly, "are you sick? Is your little wing broken?"

She put out her hand experimentally and again the pigeon shuffled out of her reach. He seemed to walk with a rather rolling gait, although she could not be certain if his awkwardness stemmed from a physical injury or simply from the precariousness of his cramped and slanted perch.

"Why," she said, "you're deathly ill; that's what's the matter with you. You've fallen and broken your wing or your little leg and you just don't know what to do, do you?"

The pigeon did not answer her.

"Here," Mrs. Patchford said, "come here." She was

reacting to the situation out of the capacity for deep
compassion and maudlin sympathy which was a part of
her emotional make-up, and she was not entirely certain
of what she would have done had the pigeon hopped into
her extended hand.

He did not do so.

"Well," she cooed, "if you won't come here I don't
know what I'll do with you, I just don't."

She straightened up and thought of walking on, but
somehow the bird's plight kept her rooted to the spot.

"Don't worry," she whispered, bending down again.
"You just stay right there and I'll go in here," pointing
at Brooks Brothers window, "and get somebody to take
care of you."

With a satisfied smile Mrs. Patchford walked reso-
lutely into the store. On her left a young man in a gray
flannel suit stood with his hands on top of a glass counter. He smiled at her.

"Good morning," he said.

"Good morning," Mrs. Patchford said in a confiden-
tial tone.

"Could I help you?" the young man said.

"Yes," Mrs. Patchford said. "There's a pigeon outside."

"I beg your pardon?"

"I was just wondering," Mrs. Patchford said, still
confidentially, leaning toward the man over the counter,
"I was just wondering if you had a telephone here."

"Why, yes," the man said, withdrawing almost unnoticeably. "I imagine it would be all right . . . if you wanted to use it, that is."

"Oh, no," Mrs. Patchford said, "I don't want to use it. You see, there's a little pigeon outside and he doesn't seem to be feeling well."

The man chuckled briefly for no apparent reason and then stopped suddenly and looked carefully at Mrs. Patchford.

"What's the matter with him?" he asked, looking about the store.

"Why," she said, lifting her eyebrows, "that's just it. I don't know. He seems to have been injured, but I don't really know what's the matter with him."

"I see," the man said, running his upper front teeth down hard over his lower lip and frowning.

A somewhat older man with steel-rimmed glasses sidled up casually next to Mrs. Patchford.

"Can I help?" he asked, looking at the younger man.

"Maybe," the man in the gray flannel suit said. "This lady wants to make a phone call about a pigeon."

The older man smiled for a moment and then looked serious again.

"A phone call, you say?"

"Yes," said Mrs. Patchford. "I was just telling this gentleman that there's a sick pigeon outside on your window ledge. I thought something should be done about it."

"Certainly," said the older man. "Just what was it you had in mind?"

"Why, I don't know, really," Mrs. Patchford said,

shrugging. "I thought maybe someone should call the SPCA."

"I see," the man said thoughtfully. "But isn't the SPCA for dogs and horses and things like that?"

"I'm not at all sure," Mrs. Patchford said. "But there should be somebody you could call." She had raised her voice just a bit.

A third man walked up. He was plump and business-like. "Everything all right?" he said.

"Yes, Charlie," the man with the steel-rimmed glasses said. "This lady just came in to tell us about a pigeon outside."

"What about it?"

"I've just told these gentlemen . . ." Mrs. Patchford began tiredly.

"Did you say a pigeon?" the new man asked.

"Yes," said the young man in the flannel suit.

"Who saw it?"

"This lady."

"Anyone else see it?"

"No," said the young man.

"No," Mrs. Patchford said. "I just came in this minute. It's outside, you see, on your ledge. I really wouldn't have bothered you but it *is* your ledge, after all, and I thought——"

"Maybe," the new man said, "we'd better all go out and take a look."

"I really don't see what good that would do," Mrs. Patchford said, with some condescension. "There's nothing to look at except this little pigeon and he seems ill, that's all. Why doesn't somebody call the SPCA?"

"We'll be glad to, madam," the plump man said, looking at her curiously. "Now just where did you think—just where did you see the pigeon?"

Mrs. Patchford turned with the merest trace of irritation and pointed to the display window behind her.

"He's right out there," she said, tightening the muscles at the corners of her mouth.

Unaccountably the young man behind the counter laughed. The others glared at him openly. He looked down and began straightening some wool-knit ties that lay on the glass counter.

"I think," said Mrs. Patchford, "that perhaps we'd *better* go take a look at him."

"Why, of course," the plump man said, shuffling in the direction of the door. The young man came out from behind the counter, the man with the steel-rimmed spectacles moved forward, and two salesmen from another part of the store moved in on the group.

Behind Mrs. Patchford's back the young man looked smugly at the two newcomers and lifted his right forefinger to his temple. He rotated the finger briefly and then pressed it to the side of his head.

Mrs. Patchford swept grandly out onto the sidewalk, followed by the five men.

"Now, then," she said grimly.

The men gathered in a small knot on the sidewalk and looked at her silently.

"It's right here," she said, directing a finger at a point on the blank, deserted ledge.

"Why," chuckled Mrs. Patchford, "that's funny. There's nothing—he's not here." She whirled frantically and searched the sidewalk, the entire store front, the curb, and the sky overhead.

"Looks like he flew away," the plump man said, looking sadly at Mrs. Patchford.

"But I can't understand it," she said. "I thought he couldn't fly."

"Well, you know," the plump man said softly, "sometimes they can."

"Yes," said Mrs. Patchford. "Well, good morning."

Behind her someone, she thought, laughed; but she could not be sure.

She had planned to buy only a skirt at Bonwit's but now she went in and bought three dresses and a pair of expensive gloves.

Afterward she had a headache and did not go to the hairdresser's at all.

3

THE INTERVIEW

*W*hen *Sarah Brigham walked into the room she* experienced a flicker of disappointment. It was a nice room but not quite what she had expected.

"Just make yourself at home," the maid said. "I'll tell Miss Prentiss you're here."

"Thank you," Sarah said, removing her gloves. Behind her, the maid fussed for a moment with an ashtray, then stepped out of the room.

"It's been rather chilly," Sarah said.

The maid came back into the room.

"Beg pardon, ma'am?"

"Oh," Sarah said, "I thought you were still here."

"Yes," said the maid absently. "I'll tell Miss Prentiss."

"Thank you," Sarah said, taking her glasses out of her handbag.

She removed her coat, placed it over the back of a chair, and looked about the room. After a moment she walked to the mantelpiece and picked up a large framed photograph of Josephine Prentiss. The maid re-entered.

"Miss Prentiss said to make yourself at home. She'll only be a minute."

"Thank you," Sarah said. "Have you been with her long?"

"No, ma'am. Only a minute."

"No, I mean—have you been employed by Miss Prentiss for a long time?"

"Oh, yes, ma'am. For a long time."

"I suppose it's quite exciting," Sarah said, "working for such a famous person."

"Yes," the maid said, "I suppose it is."

"Incidentally," Sarah said, smiling, "I'm not just being nosy. I've come to interview Miss Prentiss."

"Oh, that's all right."

"I'm going to write a story about her," Sarah explained.

"That's nice," the maid said. "There's a lot of stories about Miss Prentiss."

Lighting a cigarette, Sarah Brigham asked, "Are you happy working for her?"

"I guess so. She pays me good."

"I mean is she easy to get along with? Sometimes you can tell a great deal about a person just by the way they treat their . . . by the way they treat those who work for them."

"I suppose so," the maid said. "Yes, she's good to me. My sister gets all her old clothes."

"Your sister?"

"Yes," the maid said. "She's a thirty-eight. I'm too big. I used to be able to wear her things . . . but not any more. Not since my husband died."

"Oh?" Sarah said.

"I was smaller then. He always insisted."

"Just how did you happen to come with Miss Prentiss in the first place?"

"It was when she was working in *Springtime in Vienna*. My sister was her wardrobe mistress. She was married then."

"Your sister?" Sarah said.

"No, Miss *Prentiss*. That was the year she divorced Mr. Fontaine. They used to work together, you know."

"Yes," Sarah said, "I know."

"Twelve years it's been," the maid said, sitting down in a large chair.

"Did you know Mr. Fontaine?" Sarah said.

"Oh, yes," the maid said. "He was an easy man to know. He drank a lot."

"So I've heard," Sarah said, getting out her notebook.

"He used to cause Miss Prentiss quite a bit of trouble," the maid said, sighing. "People didn't understand him, exactly. We always had to explain him away."

Sarah rose and walked to a wall-to-wall bookcase.

"Does Miss Prentiss find time to do much reading?" she said. "She has a wonderful library here."

"No," the maid said. "She reads the papers . . . and the Bible . . . and astrology magazines and Pogo. That's about all."

"Who's reading that book on the table?" Sarah asked, and at that moment Josephine Prentiss made an entrance, sweepingly.

"Hello," she shouted, advancing toward Sarah. "So sorry I've kept you waiting."

"That's quite all right," Sarah said, offering her hand. "I'm Sarah Brigham."

"Yes, of *Woman's Home Companion,* isn't it?" Josephine appraised her visitor: small, eager, plain, no make-up.

"Ladies' Home Journal," Sarah said.

"Of course. Mildred, have you offered Miss . . . er . . ."

"Brigham," Sarah supplied.

"Have you offered Miss Brigham a drink?"

"No," the maid said. "I didn't think."

"What would you like, dear?" Josephine said.

"Oh, it really doesn't matter," Sarah said.

"Make us martinis, Mildred," Josephine said. "Several of them."

The maid left the room.

"Mildred's a dear," Josephine said softly. "A little peculiar, but a dear."

"Yes," said Sarah. "We've been speaking. She's very fond of you."

36

"Quite," Josephine said, settling herself in a large chair and waving a welcoming hand at the sofa. "Now, let's see. Just where would you like to start?"

"Well," Sarah said, "the Kramer office provided me with pictures, a biography, some other material, but I'd like to just, you know, chat with you for a while. I'd like to have you tell me all about yourself. It's the little personal touches that interest the reader."

"Well, let me see . . ." Josephine said, looking at the ceiling, anxious to begin discussing herself. She enjoyed being interviewed. "I've always wanted to be an actress, I suppose. I remember the year my family moved over here from Calcutta . . . my father was a missionary, you know."

"Yes, I'd heard."

"Well, I remember the year we all moved back here. The poor dear was in such bad health that they called him back and set him up in Boston. I remember the day he took me on his lap and looked me in the eye and said, 'Twinky . . .' He always called me by that ridiculous name," Josephine giggled.

"My father had a funny name for me, too," Sarah said.

Josephine Prentiss was almost imperceptibly taken aback. "Oh, did he?" she said.

"Yes."

"What was it?" Josephine asked politely.

"Snuggle-puff," said Sarah.

"Oh," said Josephine. "How . . . quaint!" Then, re-gathering speed, she said, "Well, my father looked me in the eye and said, 'Twinky, no matter what you do, as you go through life, remember this one thing——' "

The maid stepped into the room and said, "I think we're out of gin."

"Nonsense," Josephine said. "Some arrived this morning. It's probably out in the back hall."

"Oh, all right," Mildred said. "I'll look."

"Now, where were we?" Josephine said, looking at the Gimbels label in Sarah's coat as it lay over a nearby chair.

"You were telling me about your father," Sarah said.

"Oh, yes. Well, Daddy was a dear. You should have heard him preach a sermon. I tell you he could really put the fear of God in your heart, God bless him! He was a fine figure of a man. Tall, straight, touch of gray at the temples. My mother adored him."

"Is she . . ." Sarah asked, "are they both . . . ?"

"Dead?" Josephine said. "Yes. I'm alone now. Have been for quite a while. But I carry on. There's a great deal to live for. Did you see my last play?"

"No, I'm afraid I didn't," Sarah apologized. "I saw you in *The Fourth Commandment*, though. You were wonderful."

"That's what they all *said*. I *was* rather happy in the show, come to think of it. I believe I was in love with Stanley White at the time."

"Do you mind if I mention that in the story?" Sarah asked.

"No," Josephine said, "I suppose it's all right. It *was* in all the papers, although I wish Walter hadn't used that dreadful picture of me. I looked a million years old. It was taken the year they were wearing their hair like this, you know . . ." She gestured with her hands to her hair ". . . and I looked like Margaret Sullavan after she'd been soaked in water for three weeks. Dreadful, just dreadful. But, my dear, Stanley was a darling. An absolute darling. Ah, me . . ." She was lost for a moment in reverie.

"I always loved him myself," Sarah said. "He reminded me of a boy I went to high school with."

"Oh, *did* you?" Josephine said. "I mean . . . did he?"

"Yes," Sarah said. "The boy's name was Roland Culver. He was from Boston, too, come to think of it. I don't suppose you . . ." She paused.

"No," Josephine Prentiss said.

The maid entered with a silver tray. "Here are the drinks, Miss Prentiss." She served Sarah and Josephine martinis from the tray.

"Thank you," Sarah said, taking a sip.

"Thank you, Mildred," Josephine, drinking rather thirstily. "Oh," she said, "I needed that. Just put the tray here, dear."

"Yes, ma'am," Mildred said, placing the tray and cocktail shaker on the coffee table in front of the sofa.

"Now, let me see," Josephine pondered. "What was I saying? Don't you take notes?"

"Sometimes," said Sarah, "but I prefer to just listen. I have a good memory."

"I see," Josephine said. "Well, anyway, my father (he was from Dublin, you know) he built our home with

39

his own hands, the poor dear. The home in Calcutta, I mean. Oh, he had help, I suppose, but he directed the work himself. After Sissy (that's my sister), after Sissy and I were born he built a wing on the house instead of buying the organ that he'd wanted for such a long time. And then when Mother fell ill he built another wing. He was always doing something constructive. Well, we eventually lost the place . . ."

"How?"

"I don't know, exactly," Josephine said. "Perhaps it just flew away. That's just a little joke of mine. Yes. Well, anyway, when we came to America, Sissy and I were just two poor little waifs all alone in the great big city of Boston, and I remember Daddy took me on his lap the first night we spent in America, and said, 'Twinky, Mother is very ill, and it's just you and Sissy and myself from here on in, sweetheart.' "

"Oh," said Sarah, warmly, "did *your* father raise *you,* too?"

"I beg your pardon?" Josephine said.

"My mother died when I was fairly young," Sarah explained.

"You poor dear," Josephine said.

"I'm sorry. Go on."

"Yes. Well, Sissy and I were entered in a private school in Boston and I'll never forget the first day we showed up at the school. All the other children were quite wealthy and had just adorable clothes. Poor Sissy and I wore those horrible long black stockings that came up over our knees and I'll never forget, when we walked into the room (we were late, I think), and when we walked in all the other children laughed at us. They laughed and laughed and laughed, damn their ugly little hearts. It was dreadful. Poor Sissy burst into tears, I remember, and ran out into the hall, with me right after her."

"Oh, that's . . . tragic," Sarah said, touched.

"Yes," Josephine admitted, "it was. Sissy wouldn't go back to school for a week, but I'd be damned if they could keep me away. Oh, I was crying inside, too, but I wouldn't let on. I wouldn't give in and let those little snobs know how they'd hurt me!"

Sarah finished her drink.

"Here," Josephine said, "let me put a head on that for you." She poured Sarah and herself two more drinks. "Oh, my dear, the stories I could tell you."

"What was your mother like?" Sarah said.

"An angel," Josephine said. "An absolute angel. And what an actress! She, my dear, was the only real talent in our family. Oh, my father was magnificent, and I've had my modest success, but my mother . . . There, my dear, was the greatest thing since Duse. She had my father around her little finger. Never raised her voice, but she controlled him absolutely. And tears . . . You've never seen anyone who could cry like my mother. Phony tears, usually . . . crocodile tears . . . but she could call upon them as a weapon, a most effective weapon. I'll never forget the time (Mildred, bring some more martinis, dear), I'll never forget the time I was working in my first show, rather a long time ago, I'm afraid. Anyway, I had told Mother I had a very important role, the part of a great lady, because Mother wasn't too keen about my getting into show business to begin with, but she finally had decided that if I could possibly become a star, a very important star, that, well, it might be all right. Well, I had told her I had practically the lead in this production, and I made her promise that she wouldn't come to see the play on opening night. Well, I didn't even make my entrance until the middle of the second act, and when I did I simply walked up to a man standing under a street lamp—I don't think you'd remember the play—I walked up to this man and said, 'Pardon me, but do you have a cigarette?' I remember my hair was stringy and I was wearing a tattered skirt, with a split up the side. A pathetic little prostitute is what I really was. Well, my dear, I delivered this one line and then stood there, looking out over the footlights smoking a cigarette and flirting with this man.

"He ignored me, actually. Walked right away from me. Well, I'm standing there and suddenly my heart turned right over in my body. There, sitting in the first row, was my mother. The man, I forget who it was now, turned to me and said, 'Run along home, little girl. I think your mother is looking for you.' Well, my mother gasped! You could hear her all over the theater. And then she started to cry, and I started to cry. I don't even remember walking off the stage, I was so ashamed. I refused to come out of my dressing room until everyone had left the theater and I didn't go home for two days."

42

Josephine Prentiss' eyes were tear-filled now at the memory.

"Was your mother angry?" Sarah whispered.

"No. That's the tragic part of it. The poor dear was terribly displeased, of course, but she wouldn't let me see it. She was ashamed of me, and I was ashamed of myself, but God bless her, she threw her arms around me when I walked in and kissed me and held me and told me that she was very sure that one day I would be the very greatest actress the theater had ever known."

With cocktail shaker refilled the maid entered. She walked to the coffee table and filled both glasses.

"Thank you, dear," Josephine said.

"Miss Prentiss," said little Sarah Brigham emotionally, "you *are* a great actress. I hope you'll forgive me. My eyes seem to have clouded up." She laughed with embarrassment.

"Thank you, dear," Josephine said. "You're very sweet. Well" (they lifted their glasses toward each other), "*c'est la guerre*. Did you say you were from Boston?"

"Well, partly," Sarah said. "We lived there for a few years. When Mother died we moved to Chicago."

"I see," Josephine said. "I loved Boston . . . with its winding streets and its straight people."

"That's a wonderfully descriptive line," Sarah said. "I think I will make a note of that." She fumbled in her purse, took out a note pad and pencil and jotted a few words.

"Do you think," said Josephine, "that the readers of *Woman's Home Companion*——"

"*Ladies' Home Journal.*"

"Of course. Do you think your readers would be interested more in little stories about me than they would in my comments about the theater?"

"Well, I imagine we can use some of both. Just say anything that comes into your head . . . the way you have been."

"Does it seem warm in here to you?" Josephine said. She opened her dress a bit at the neck and fanned herself with a handkerchief. "Mildred, darling, would you open a window or create a draft or something? These autumn afternoons are very much like . . . *summer* afternoons . . . aren't they?"

"A little," agreed Sarah, sipping her martini.

"Well," Josephine said, "let me see. Oh, yes. My first play. Let me see, it was back in nineteen . . . well, the date isn't important."

"It is to me," Sarah said.

"It's not to me," Josephine said.

"Very well," Sarah said, sipping her drink.

"I'll never forget that play," Josephine said. "I think that was the company . . . Yes, of course. It was *The Willow Tree.* Ralph Forbes or somebody was in the cast. No, it was Ralph Graves. I remember I had a love affair with the boy who died in the third act. You wouldn't remember his name. I remember I brought him home for dinner one night. He was tremendously wealthy. His father owns half of Canada or something. Anyway, I was mad about him, simply mad. I called Mother in the afternoon and told her I was bringing him home to dinner and when Richard . . . that was his name . . . when Richard and I arrived it was dreadful. Everything went wrong. First of all, my father answered the door in his stocking feet and suspenders."

"How dreadful," Sarah said.

"Yes, terribly," Josephine said. "We were trying to be so fancy, you see. Well, my mother had forgotten to tell Daddy about my bringing Richard home and it turned out that Daddy had invited his brother to dinner. It was his black-sheep brother. He was always getting into scrapes and Daddy was always getting him out of them. Well, this night Uncle Fred was a little drunk and, oh, my dear, I'll never forget it. He sat at the table and twice he belched right out loud and poor Mother, God bless her, the poor angel, was so embarrassed for herself and for me that she dropped the roast when she brought it into the dining room and she didn't know what to do, the poor darling. Daddy picked it up and took it back to the kitchen, and if it was just us we would have eaten it, but with Richard there we didn't know what to do. I think we just had soup and then Uncle Fred got into an argument with Richard and Richard went home. I was so terribly in love with him, you see, but I never had the heart to . . . speak to him . . . much . . . after that day. He married someone else, a society girl, a few months later."

Sarah blew her nose sniffingly. "Oh, dear," she said, "I'm so sorry. I don't know why I'm acting like this.

It's just that you tell these stories as if they had just happened yesterday, Miss Prentiss, and I . . . I don't know. Something very much like that happened to me once and you just seemed to strike some kind of responsive chord. I'm so ashamed." She finished her drink.

"Nonsense, my dear," Josephine said. "A good cry never hurt anyone. I think you're a darling, acting like this. I really do."

"The boy in my life when I was about that age," Sarah passed on, ". . . the age you were in that story, I mean . . . was a very wealthy boy whose father owned the building we lived in in Chicago. Harry Ryan was his name. He played football, and I was the editor of our college paper. I remember I interviewed him one day and he invited me to have dinner with him. I . . . I wore braces on my teeth at the time, and even then I had to wear these horrible glasses . . . and I waited for him for two hours and then——"

"There, there, dear," Josephine said, patting her shoulder. "Don't you worry. Those football players are never worth it. Not a bit of it, you poor darling."

"Oh, I don't give a damn *now*," Sarah said, "but he never showed up. I didn't hear from him at all after that. Ohhh, God. The only reason I'm explaining all this is so that you'll understand how close your stories strike to home. You've had such a tragic life, evidently."

"Yes, I have," Josephine confessed.

"And sometimes it just seems that life is so terribly full of tragedy for so many of us that . . . I don't know

. . . sometimes you wonder what is the purpose of it all."

"Daddy knew what the purpose was, the poor angel. He raised Sissy and me to love and to fear God and to do the best we could for the most people."

"He must have been a fine man," Sarah said warmly. "I haven't been to church in years."

"That's too bad, my dear. It can be a great comfort. A great comfort."

"Oh, do you go?" Sarah said.

"No, not since Daddy died."

"Why not?"

"I don't know, really. I have nothing against it. I just seem to be up so late on Saturday night."

"I suppose your personal life must be very exciting . . . parties and things." Sarah said, trying to brighten the mood.

"Well," said Josephine, "there aren't so many parties, but . . . quite a few . . . things."

"When was it you met Mr. Fontaine?" Sarah said.

"Oh, Henry?" Josephine said. "Quite a few years ago. We worked together in *The Lost Chord*. We were married while we were touring. I think he proposed in Buffalo . . . and then in Cleveland . . ."

"That's where you were married?"

"No, that's where he backed out."

"Oh," Sarah said.

"He changed his mind in St. Louis and we were married in Los Angeles. Henry wasn't a bad sort, the poor dear, although he drank a great deal."

Sarah rose unsteadily and walked to a tray of cigarettes on a lamp table. "Where is he now, do you know?"

"No," Josephine said. "He floated away about seven years ago. Last I heard he was in Honolulu or Cuba."

"What was he doing?"

"I think he had gotten into Rum . . . or vice versa."

Sarah laughed heartily. "When you met him, was it love at first sight?" she said.

"I don't think so. You might say his interest in me was purely paternal."

"Paternal?"

"He wanted to become a father."

"Oh," Sarah said, returning to the sofa. "It all sounds so romantic and exciting. Sometimes I get so sick of *my* life. By contrast it seems so drab, so dull. The same thing day after day. I'd love to be like you—to live dangerously, as the saying goes—to do something . . . to be somebody's mistress or something." She emptied her glass and poured herself another. "Tell me another of your stories."

"Well, let me see," Josephine said. "Oh, yes. I did want to tell you about the time when Sissy and I were looking for work on Broadway. We took a little room in a dingy hotel just off Times Square, and day after day we tramped the streets, looking for a walk-on, a small role, anything. Sissy, the poor dear, as I remember didn't even have a decent coat. We had this one nice coat between us; Mother had made it, as I recall. That's right. My mother made it. It was heavy red wool with a black velvet collar and it was really darling. Well,

when we were looking for work in some cheap show
or in a small agent's office we could walk in together
because Sissy's old brown coat was good enough for
that sort of thing, but when we were trying to make an
impression on somebody *important* the poor little waif
would have to stay home in that dingy little room in
that run-down hotel (I remember the bellboys were unspeakable), and there'd she'd sit, the angel, looking out
the window, looking up Forty-seventh Street till she'd
see me coming back, and I'd look up at her, sitting up
there on the third floor looking down at me (she was
only about sixteen at the time) and, honestly, it would
break your heart to see that dear little face, with those
big brown eyes, looking down like a puppy. Yes, for
all the world like a dear little puppy that had been left
behind. And then if I'd found something I'd smile and
nod, 'Yes,' and by the time I'd gotten upstairs to the
room she'd be delirious with joy. And if I hadn't been
able to find anything I'd shake my head, 'No,' and we'd
sit up there in that damned dingy room and hold onto
each other and cry. And then I'd let her put on the red
wool coat with the black velvet collar and she, poor
angel—I remember it was just a little bit too large for
her—she'd put it on and out she'd go, and I'd sit in the
window and watch her as she went off up the street with
her pretty yellow hair gleaming . . . and her little face
lifted eagerly and so bravely. Oh, my dear, it," crying,
"it's so sad to think of it now. I tell you——"

"Where is Sissy now?" Sarah asked breathily.

"She's living in Denver," Josephine said, sighing.

"Her husband is head of one of the Sears-Roebuck stores there or something."

"Oh, it's all so very touching," Sarah said. "How brave you are, Miss Prentiss. How very brave to fight your way up out of poverty and sickness and tragedy to your present position. This is going to be a marvelous story to write. I can't wait to get to my typewriter. . . . Does your maid have any more martinis ready?"

"There's more in here," Josephine Prentiss said. She poured from the cocktail shaker, filling Sarah's glass and then her own.

"I can't wait to sit down and begin working on this thing," Sarah said. "The material is perfect. Just fascinating. I suppose you've been telling these stories all your life and you're a bit tired of them, but to me——"

"Oh, not at all, my dear. I get quite carried away hearing them myself, I really do. We actresses need only an audience, you know. We thrive on attention and approval and adulation."

"Oh, I understand perfectly," Sarah said. "In fact, I haven't felt at all as if this has been an interview, if you know what I mean. Sometimes it has seemed more like a . . . a performance . . . and I've felt like a spectator. Then again I've felt as if I were chatting with an old, old friend—I hope you'll forgive me."

"Don't be silly, dear. There's nothing to forgive."

"I suppose I've been drinking a bit too much," Sarah said. "I usually don't act like this."

"Nonsense. It's good for you. I remember one time when——"

"You see, I usually don't drink much at all. It's so
. . . funny."

"Of course," Josephine said. "As I was saying, I
remember the time when Daddy and——"

"Oh, your *father*," cried Sarah. "He sounds so much
like my own!"

"Is that right?"

"Yes, terribly, the poor thing. Our mothers were
nothing alike. Yours sounds like a saint, but my mother
was a . . . a . . . she ran a speak-easy."

"A speak-easy?"

"Yes," Sarah said, making a face. "I hated her. Does
that sound awful? She was beautiful and exciting and
everything that I'm not, and she was cheap and coarse,
too. For all her faults my father adored her. She ruined
his life."

"Dreadful," said Josephine, looking on dully.

"Yes," Sarah insisted, "it was. We lived up over a
restaurant on the South Side (my father sold shoes and
was trying to write a novel on the side), and my mother
had an affair with the man who owned the restaurant
and the two of them decided to open a speak-easy . . .
it was in the first days of Prohibition, you see. My poor
father had a lot of respectable friends, poor people, but
respectable, and finally he got so embarrassed when they
would come around that he stopped inviting them. He
would just sit up in the apartment at the dining-room
table at night, with his pathetic little papers and things
spread out in front of him, trying to write something
worthwhile. He never did though. He had no talent

whatsoever, the poor angel. But he was only happy, I think, when he was up there trying to write something, sitting there amongst his dictionaries and thesauruses and clippings and rejection slips—and then my mother would come upstairs with that unspeakable man—and the two of them would drink and carry on right in front of my father. Ohhh." She recoiled at the memory. "And right in front of me. I couldn't ever bring boys home because of all the fighting and drinking. I remember one time a boy walked me home from school, and I liked him very much, and when we got to the back gate out in the alley I don't know what went through my mind but I didn't want to say good-by to him and go upstairs alone. I wanted to keep him with me. I guess I was in love with him . . . so I said, 'Would you like to come upstairs for a Coca-Cola or something?' and he said, 'Why, yes, I suppose I would,' so I said, 'Well, all right, come on up,' and we walked up the back stairs, and I thought my mother would be out (my father was at the store. It was a dingy little store near the Stratford Theatre, just up a ways from the corner of Sixty-third and Halsted Street— I don't think you'd know just where— But it was right next door to a candy store and my father used to bring me home little things from the candy store sometimes, pink and yellow bonbons). Well, anyway, this boy and I walked up the back stairs. We were holding hands and laughing and for a minute I thought he was going to kiss me while I was standing there putting my key into the door, but I guess he saw my braces and changed his mind or something . . . but there we were, laughing and having a really wonderful time. He was so tall and thin and sweet and shy, I just loved him. I was never happier and then I opened the back door and the lights were out in the kitchen and we both stepped in and . . . ohhhh——" She sobbed uncontrollably.

"There, there, now," Josephine said. "What happened? It'll do you good to go on."

"We stepped into the kitchen," Sarah said thickly, "and I turned on the light over the table and there on the *floor* was my mother, lying right there on the linoleum, drunk! With her kimono open and nothing to cover her body. Lying right there on the linoleum, you understand—in the kitchen—half-naked . . . like a wild animal . . . and there were broken bottles all around. I guess she and that man had had a fight or something, but there she was . . . Oh, God! It was awful. I wanted to die. I told the boy right there while he stood there looking at me and then at her . . . I told him I was sorry and that I wanted to kill myself. I wanted to run to him and put my arms around him and beg him to take me away, far away, to someplace where it was warm and green and the sun was shining—but I couldn't ask him to do that. We were just two children in school and he was so pathetically embarrassed." She laughed a little hysterically. "I remember he even laughed, he was so embarrassed. He tried to laugh it off! He laughed a little and said, 'Oh, don't worry, Sarah. It's all right. My father drinks a little too. It happens in the best of families. Think nothing of it.' And then he said, 'Well,

I guess I'll be running along,' and when I saw him backing out of the kitchen like a big, confused puppy I wanted to hold him, to make him stay. I needed something to hold onto, I guess. It was so confusing. Because at the same time I wanted him to go away and never come back. I didn't ever want to see him . . . ever again. Or else I wanted to run away with him . . . but before I would have gone . . . I wanted to walk over to that drunken *slut* lying on the linoleum, snoring, and stamp on her face with my heels. I wanted to kill her! Oh, God . . . God . . . God . . . God . . . God." There was a long pause while the two women sat, not looking at each other, each absorbed in her own thoughts.

Mildred entered, whispering. "Was there anything the matter, Miss Prentiss?"

"No, Mildred," Josephine said, "nothing. We . . . we've just been sitting here, conducting an interview, Miss Brigham and I. Everything is fine."

Sarah, gathering herself together: "I'm so sorry, Miss Prentiss. I guess I've overstayed my welcome."

"Why, no . . ." Josephine started to protest.

"No, it's all right," Sarah said. "I have to be running along anyway. You've given me a great deal of material, and I can fill in the rest from the biography. I think I need a bit of fresh air." She rose and put on her coat and gloves. Then she put the hat on so that it was rather askew. Her purse was hanging open. "I don't remember when anything went to my head like . . . those martinis," she said. "I do hope you'll forgive me. I've got to get back to the office now."

"Do you?" Josephine asked. She felt a little drunk.

"Yes. I'm expecting a gentleman caller there. He's taking me to dinner. Thank you very much, Miss Prentiss. If there's anything else I need I'll——" She broke off and walked out of the apartment.

"Mildred," said Josephine Prentiss quietly, "I have been upstaged."

4

"I HOPE I'M NOT INTRUDING"

The first inkling they had was when the woman at the other table held the hand of the man who had just stood up. "Don't tell me," they heard him say, freeing his hand, and then he began to walk toward them.

"Oh, God," Gus said, "here we go again."

As he approached, walking with that great dignity that only the slightly intoxicated are able to muster, the man smiled thinly. When he reached their table he stood stiffly, waiting to be addressed. They all kept their heads down and began talking again.

"I don't see that the dress itself mattered so much," Gus said. "It's just that we discussed the whole thing yesterday. I *told* her she looked better in something tight and clinging, ya know? And so tonight, wham, here she comes back again with the same dress that started the trouble."

"I didn't think it was the *same* dress," Gordon said.

"Well, if it wasn't it photographed the same, so my point is still good."

"You say you mentioned it to her?" Gordon's wife said.

"Sure," Gus said. "After the show the other night we had coffee. I did like twenty minutes on the dress bit and she says fine, she'll take care of it, and then tonight we're right back where we started from."

"We should have caught it in rehearsal," Gordon said.

"Oh, I noticed it all right," Gus said, "but I didn't want to bother you while you were busy, and then too sometimes she'll rehearse in one dress and work in another, ya know?"

"Excuse me," said the man standing in the aisle. They all looked up and pretended to be surprised that he was there. He looked about forty-five, Midwestern, well-to-do. His suit was gray, conservative. His glasses were rimless. He looked like a speaker at a Kiwanis luncheon. He did not appear to be at all embarrassed.

"Excuse me," he repeated, "I hope I'm not intruding."

"Not at all," said Gordon.

There was a pause.

"Gordon Lester?"

"That's right," Gordon said, feeling for his fountain pen automatically. Perhaps an autograph would . . .

"I saw your show tonight."

"That's fine," Gus said. "Just fine. We hope you enjoyed it. Now, anyway, Ruth, when I told Billie she ought to get down to see Florence Lustig or somebody about some dresses, why, she thought——"

"I'm from Baltimore," the man said.

Gus stopped talking and looked at him. "All right," he said.

Gordon and Ruth put their heads down and concentrated on their scrambled eggs. Gus looked vainly for the headwaiter.

"Saw the show tonight at the hotel," the man said. "On TV, that is."

"Was there something we could do for you?" Gordon said.

"Why, no, nothing in particular," the man said, "although there *is* something I'd like to talk to you about. My wife and I watch the program all the time and I—listen, I hope I'm not intruding or anything."

"It isn't that," Gus said, "but if it's a business matter or something, Mr. Lester would be happy to have you get in touch with him at the office."

"Oh, I don't want to bother anybody during working hours," the man said. Then he turned and pulled an empty chair toward the table. "May I sit down?" he said.

Ruth stared at Gordon helplessly. Gus pursed his lips. "Certainly," he said.

"Fine," the man said, seating himself. "I'm from Baltimore. Arnold's the name. J. K. Arnold."

Gus nodded.

"Your name?" the man said.

"Mr. Werner," Gus said.

"Have a little proposition for you," the man said.

"Fine," Gus said, taking out a pencil, writing a number on a piece of paper. "Look, this is the number at the office. Give us a call any time after one in the afternoon. Be happy to talk to you."

"Tell you the truth," the man said, "I'm leaving in the morning. Besides, you fellas probably have enough to do putting your shows together without me taking up your time. Here's my card."

"Thank you," Gus said, taking it.

"Yes, sir," said the man. "We get a mighty big kick out of your program there, Mr. Lester. A *mighty* big kick. I tell my wife I'll divorce her if she doesn't stop staying up every night to watch you, but she says she don't care. She just loves that damn program. Tell you the truth, she loves it a darn sight more'n I do. Meaning no offense, you understand, but some nights are better than others."

Ruth bristled, putting down her fork.

"Gordon," she said, "have you heard from Agnes?"

"Why, no," Gordon said. "Just that letter we got around Christmas. Nothing since."

"That's funny," Ruth said. "She's usually very good about writing."

"Say, listen," said Arnold, "I'm not interrupting anything here, am I? I mean I came over here on a business proposition."

Gus leaped at the bait.

"Fine," he said. "Then you just give us a call at this number any afternoon after about one or one-thirty and I'll be happy to take care of you. I'm Mr. Lester's manager."

"Oh, yeah?" said the man.

"That's right."

"Well, that's all right," the man said, "except for the little fact that I happen to be leaving town in the morning. But I'll get right down to business here. I've got an idea that I think you might be very, *very* interested in, Mr. Lester."

"Thank you," Gordon said, because he could not think of anything else to say.

"We watch you every night down there, by God," the man said. "You're a much younger-lookin' fella than I thought you were, judging from TV, I mean. It don't do you justice."

"Thank you," Gordon said.

"No, sir," the man said. "On TV you look kinda fat, but in person you look a lot better."

Ruth turned, craning her neck trying to catch the attention of a captain.

There was a pause.

"You were saying something about a business matter," Gus said softly.

"Oh, yes," the man said. "That's what I wanted to talk to you folks about, but I certainly didn't want to intrude on your little gathering here."

They all looked at their plates.

"It's just," the man continued, "that I don't think

61

you TV fellas ever look down your nose at a little commercial business, do you?"

"No," Gus said.

"Well, fine and dandy," the man said, "because that's the area I'm talking in."

"Maybe you'd better take it up with the network," Gordon said, "if it's that sort of thing. We just *do* the program, we don't *sell* it."

"Maybe *you'd* better take it up with the network," the man said, showing the first sign of truculence. He withdrew another card from his vest. "My card," he said, handing it to Gus.

"You already gave me one," Gus said.

"That's all right," the man said. "All the better."

Ruth gasped with audible impatience.

"Like I say," the man said, "I'll be leaving in the morning but I'll be at the Waldorf till about eleven-thirty. I think it might be a very good idea if you boys had the network call me about this little matter."

"All right," Gus said.

"I mean, I don't want to impose or anything, but you fellas are in the same kinda business we're all in, aren't you? The business of making a buck?"

"That's right," Gus said.

At this admission the man evidenced vast satisfaction. "Well, then," he chuckled, "you just have them call J. K. Arnold in the morning at the Waldorf and everything'll be just fine. Got a few ideas that might help that program of yours, Gordon-boy."

He rose to his feet, swaying slightly.

"My apologies," he said grandly, "to the lady. Mrs. Lester, is it?"

Ruth smiled confirmation.

"Fine," he said. "Very happy to meet you. See you TV or movie fellas out with a pretty girl, ya don't know *whose* wife it might be."

At this moment Ruth happened to catch the eye of the headwaiter. She looked at him sternly, then nodded toward Arnold. The waiter made an apologetic face, stepping forward.

"May I help you, sir?" he said to Arnold.

"No, you may not," the man answered. "I was talking to my friends here."

"All right," said Gus, getting as much finality into his voice as possible. "Thanks for the information. You'll hear from us."

"You know Gordon Lester?" Arnold suddenly demanded of the captain.

"Certainly, sir."

"Well, take good care of him and his friends here. They're all right. Ol' Gordon ain't the *funniest* guy on television, but he *does* have the prettiest wife."

Laughing softly, Arnold retreated.

Gus carefully tore his two cards into small pieces.

Back at his table Arnold addressed his wife rudely. "Come on, Sal. Let's hit the road."

"Sit down till the check comes," his wife said. "I hope you didn't bother them over there."

"Bother?" Arnold said. "Are you joking? Nobody is ever bothered when you offer 'em a chance to make a

buck. Say, that reminds me, I gotta go back there and get Lester's autograph for the kids."

"Jack, sit down, will you?"

"All right. All right. I'll sit down. Say, captain."

"Yes, sir?"

"Tell Mr. Lester to step over here on his way out, will ya? I want to get his autograph for my niece and nephew."

5

THE CATS

When she heard the first rumble of thunder Blanche touched the tip of her tongue to the back of her upper front teeth, making the traditional sound of annoyance. Then she left the kitchen and walked to the living room and closed the windows.

A thin, spattered film of water lay on each sill. She wiped all of it away with the end of her apron and stood for a moment looking absently out at the traffic on Seventy-eighth Street. A taxi had double-parked and two middle-aged women had gotten out and were standing in the drizzling rain, taking too much time to pay the driver. Several cars were lined up and there was much honking of horns.

"Come on, 'ere," somebody called from down the street.

Blanche turned away from the window, walked to the television set, and turned it on. After a moment a voice said "—twice the work in half the time. And remember, it cleans as it scours as it shines." Before the picture even came up Blanche turned the station-selector knob. As she did so, a woman's face came fuzzily into view on the glass plate.

"—certainly be a conversation piece," the woman was saying. It was Jinx. Blanche took a package of cigarettes out of her apron pocket, lighted one, and sat down on a hassock.

Jinx put aside the delicate glass bowl she was holding and smiled broadly, away from the camera. The picture widened to include another woman. Blanche giggled. It was Mrs. Hollis.

"—delighted you could take the time out to visit us this afternoon," Jinx was saying.

"Thanks," Mrs. Hollis said, a little breathlessly, "but I'm so sorry I was late. Honestly, I just *couldn't* get a cab, and then you know crosstown traffic."

Both women laughed and so did Blanche.

"If I didn't call you, you *still* be asleep," said Blanche to the television set. She sat listening to Jinx and Mrs. Hollis talk about Mrs. Hollis' new novel, about her newspaper column, and about her French poodle. At the mention of the dog's name Blanche wrinkled her nose in displeasure.

"—a successful career woman, a housewife, and a mother," Jinx said. "It's truly remarkable how you do it all."

66

"Psshh," Blanche said softly.

At that moment Mr. Hollis walked through the living room. Blanche sat upright, then stood, frightened, and tried to hide the cigarette. Mr. Hollis pretended not to notice.

"I won't be home for dinner, Blanche," he said.

"Yes, sir," Blanche said. "You want me to tell Mrs. Hollis anything?" As she said it she pointed to the screen.

Mr. Hollis did not become interested.

"Just tell her I won't be home for dinner," he repeated.

Blanche knew precisely what Mrs. Hollis did when she left the comfortable brownstone on Seventy-eighth Street, East, but she had never arrived at a really clear understanding as to what Mr. Hollis did or where he went or even, exactly, what he was.

"I don't know," she had said to her sister, coming down on the Fifth Avenue bus out of Harlem early in the morning. "He read a lot and he drink a lot and he talk to a lot of important people, but I'll be go-ta-hell if I know just what he do."

"Maybe," her sister had ventured with a knowing chuckle, "he just sit home and count the money Mrs. Hollis make."

"No," Blanche had said. "He got money in his own name. He ain't one of them gigolo husbands. I know he ain't that, but I jes' don't know what he *is*."

"What he and Mis' Hollis talk about him doin'?"

"Well, when they ain't fightin' they talk about plays

and TV shows and like that. He got somethin' to do with show business, I guess, but he's pretty close-mouthed."

Now, standing before her, pulling on his gloves, Mr. Hollis said, "Brucie get off all right this morning?"

"Yes, sir," Blanche said. "He ate good and they picked him up right on time."

"Good," Mr. Hollis said and then, with no other word, walked out of the house.

When she heard the downstairs door click Blanche sat on the hassock again and looked at the television set. Jinx and Mrs. Hollis were talking about earrings.

Blanche sat motionless for several minutes, watching them, and then the back doorbell rang in a shave-and-a-haircut pattern, twice.

"Keep your shirt on," Blanche said as she crossed the spacious kitchen. It had to be Carter.

It was.

"You all wet, man," she said when she saw him.

"I'll live," Carter said, smiling broadly. "Mr. Hollis up yet?"

"You missed him. He jes' went out."

Carter stepped in, wiping moisture from the back of his brown neck.

"Whee-hoo," he said. "It's really whalin' out there."

"Don't look too bad out to me," Blanche said.

"No," said Carter, "that's 'cause you lookin' at it from inside."

"You remember the eggplant?" Blanche said as Carter placed the two shopping bags on the kitchen table.

"Yep," he said, pointing to one of the bags, "and it's the craziest, if you dig eggplant."

They worked in silence for a few minutes, putting things away, and then Carter said, "Hey, how about puttin' down some coffee?"

"All right," Blanche said.

"Oop-shoop," said Carter, getting out two cups and saucers.

"You goin' call the cleaners?" Blanche said.

"Salt peanuts, salt peanuts," Carter sang softly. "I already did. They goofed."

"What?"

"Stuff won't be ready till tomorrow."

When the coffee was ready Carter drank it eagerly. It burned his throat a little.

"Cool," Carter said. "You order ice yet?"

"Not yet," Blanche said.

"How many people be here tonight?"

"I don't know. Maybe fifty."

"Ouch," said Carter. "They'll be whalin' all night." Then he said, "You know, Blanche, if you wasn't so fat I'd like to——"

"Aw, you shut up," Blanche said, laughing heartily with embarrassment.

Carter carefully washed and dried his cup and saucer. "I'm goin' up and play a little," he said.

"Don't you fool around up there too long."

"Mokay," said Carter.

He walked up the thickly carpeted, winding staircase

to the living room, pausing at the first landing to listen to Blanche splashing water in the kitchen. Then he stepped up to the liquor cabinet opposite the false fireplace and poured himself a good drink of straight rye whisky. Downing it quickly in four short gulps, he carefully replaced the bottle, put the glass in the pocket of his suède jacket, and sat down at the piano.

With his left hand, low on the keyboard, he played an E-flat octave. Against it in the treble he played a straight A chord. At the fine, stark, dramatic quality of the combination he smiled broadly.

"Blanche," he called at the top of his voice.

"What?" faintly.

"Man, that thing you showed me sounds *fine!*"

Cursing the stiffness of his fingers, he began to play again, trying first the blues, with the modern changes. Instead of playing the straight B-flat chord all the way through the first three measures, he changed the chord on each beat, playing slow, lush tenths, going from B-flat to C minor to D minor and then back again. With the right hand he played a traditional blues phrase, humming softly and tapping gently with his foot on the sustaining pedal; not enough to sustain the chords and run one into the other, but just enough to get a pounding, echo-y beat from the hollow parts of the piano.

Blanche listened to him for ten minutes, then, after she had put the clothes in the automatic washer, she went upstairs and sat next to him on the piano bench.

"Show me those chords to 'Lover Man,' " Carter said, sliding off the seat.

Blanche positioned herself and straightened her skirt.

"You use like a D minor to start here," she said, "and you play the left hand like this." She hit a D and G simultaneously in the lower register. Carter shivered in delight at the rich, pleasant dissonance.

"Crazy," he said.

Blanche closed her eyes and began to sing quietly in a throaty voice. When she got to the bridge of the song Carter slid back on the bench and began to play fill-in notes with his right hand.

"Yeah," he said, appreciatively as she altered the melody in the last eight bars, ad-libbing a new line, but in perfect agreement with the composer's harmonies.

"Hi," Bruce said.

They whirled and then looked at each other like trapped conspirators. Blanche paused and then said, "Yes, you're right, Carter. This piano *does* need tuning. Brucie, how come you ain't in school?"

"I didn't want to go," said Bruce, twirling his leather pilot's hat.

He was sitting at the head of the stairs, looking at them pleasantly. "Don't stop playing."

"We weren't playing," Carter said. "We just were testing the piano. How come you ain't in school? You got picked up and everything."

"Oh, I *went*," said Bruce, "but I just walked in one door and out the other. I didn't want to go to class today."

"How come?" Blanche said.

"I don't know," Bruce said. "I didn't have my homework done, and I just didn't feel like it. Is my father home?"

"No," Carter said, "and it's a good thing for you he ain't."

"No, it isn't," Bruce said. "Go on play some more."

"I got work to do," Blanche said.

"Then how come you were playing?"

"We was testing the piano."

"You don't have to *sing* to test the piano, do you?"

"No," Carter admitted. "You don't *have* to exactly, but it helps."

"Test it some more then," Bruce said, taking off his rubbers. "I want to hear you."

"But we got more important things to do, boy," Blanche said.

"Then why weren't you doing them?"

"What you gonna do when your mother finds out you ditchin' school?" said Carter, trying to change the subject.

"She won't find out for a long time," Bruce said.

"What makes you think she won't?" Carter said.

"*You're* not going to tell her, are you?" said Bruce, looking directly at Carter and then at the piano.

"Why, no," Carter said. "I guess I'm not, but she'll find out some time."

"Maybe she won't," said Bruce. Then in a business-like voice he added, "If you don't tell her either, Blanche, I won't tell her that you and Carter were playing the piano and singing."

Blanche laughed.

"Listen to him," she said. "Brucie, you're makin' a federal case out of this thing."

"Sing something else," Bruce said. "Please."

"Maybe," suggested Carter, "you better do it, Blanche."

Blanche looked from the man to the boy, then sat down.

"What would you like to hear?" she said.

"Anything you want," Bruce said. "I like to listen to you. I'd lots rather listen to you right now than be in school."

"All right," Blanche said, sighing.

She hit a G seventh chord and looked at the ceiling for inspiration.

"My funny valentine," she sang slowly, her voice low, "sweet, comic valentine. You make me smile with my heart."

Bruce put his chin on his knees and wrapped his arms around his calves.

"Your looks are laughable," she sang, smiling warmly at Bruce in the mirror, "unphotographable, but you're my favorite work of art."

"Crazy," whispered Carter, tapping his foot on the carpet very slowly.

It began to rain again and the shy, sad whisper of the rain on the windows gave to the piano a sort of warm-fireplace, golden quality. The three were figures huddling for warmth.

"Is your figure less than Greek?" Blanche sang. "Is

your mouth a little weak? When you open it to speak
. . . are you smart?"

The braces on Brucie's teeth glinted dully in the light
from the one lamp at the far end of the room. He leaned
forward eagerly; Blanche was singing softly, almost in-
audibly. Her fingers paused over a plaintive chord and
Carter sweetly hummed a low note of harmony.

Outside taxies swished lazily past the house. The
sound of their wet tires seemed part of the music. From
a million miles away the city added dreamily to the
orchestra, with ships in the river lowing like the ghosts
of blind beasts, the muffled clatter of the Third Avenue
El filling in a contrapuntal feathery staccato, and now
and then the faint English trumpet of an auto horn seeming, by its very remoteness, to make the piano and voice
in the room intensely close and personal.

Blanche's eyes were closed now and her head was
thrown slightly back. She was still keeping a slow, steady
beat with her fingers, but the voice lagged behind tan-
talizingly, like the pouring of rich honey, seeming now
to be almost out of synchronization with the music, now
to be catching up in a way that pulled Bruce forward,
chewing the piece of gum that was in his mouth in the
rhythm of the song, his head lifting regularly, his chin
still braced on his knees.

"Don't change a hair for me," Blanche sang and
Bruce loved her, feeling loved in his inadequacies.

"Not if you care for me," she whispered, and he felt
fierce and loyal.

"Stay, little valentine, stay!"

Tenderly, Blanche fingered, as if on a harp, a rippling trio of chords. Carter hummed, a faint wisp of a smile in his eyes, which were fastened on the carpet. Bruce blew his nose.

"Each day is Valentine's day." A clock ticked somewhere cozily.

When the last chord had died away they all sat motionless for perhaps five seconds and then Bruce said, "That was beautiful, Blanche. I like that song."

"Thank you," Blanche said.

"Yep," said Carter, chuckling. "This is *all right!*" He looked at their reflections in the wall mirror behind the piano. "Here we are: three cats really swingin'!"

6

THE SCRIBBLER

Stanley Moss was a small man. He was getting bald. He was forty-seven years old. His wife had great contempt for him.

"You're a lousy fag, practically," she said to him once.

He had struck her then.

She was so surprised she wept and then that night they had made love. It had been like it was when they were first married. It had been strange.

But other than that one night, they had not had a good relationship for many years. Florence was five years younger than Stanley. She was almost fat, but she was attractive in a cheap way. Her hair was peroxide-blonde and her nails were always kept red, although they were not always clean. She wore a lot of perfume and liked to drink beer. The combination of the smell of beer and the smell of perfume made her irresistible to many of the men she met in bars.

They lived in a run-down but not too unpleasant building on the West side. Stanley worked at Macy's in the basement hardware section. Sometimes he would get so angry thinking of Florence that he would stand behind his counter looking at the blades of kitchen knives, and sometimes he would grip the handle of a sharp knife and make an ugly face. He was basically, though, a mild man.

One hot Friday evening in late summer he came home to find the apartment empty. The bed had not been made and there were dirty dishes in the sink.

He watched television for a while and then went down the street to Riker's and had dinner, which consisted of Irish stew, apple pie, a glass of milk, and a cup of coffee.

When he got back to the apartment there was still no sign of Florence.

He walked over to the phone table and dialed a number.

"Hello, Dora? This is Stanley. Fine, thanks. Dora, is Flo still with you? She said she'd be home at seven o'clock. What? Oh, that's funny. No, it's nothing important. She probably just got tied up somewhere. Yes. All right. Thanks, Dora. 'Bye."

He hung up viciously, looked at his watch, rose, and paced the floor. Lunging for the phone, he dialed another number. After a moment:

"Hello, Charlie. How are you? This is Stanley Moss.

Yes. Say, I don't suppose you've seen *Mrs.* Moss, have you? Sometimes she stops in with her sister in the—oh? About how long ago? I see. What? No, nothing's wrong. I *thought* she might have stopped in at your place for a drink, that's all. Yes. All right, Charlie. Thank you."

At that moment he heard a scuffling sound from the hall outside the apartment and the sound of a woman's laughter. Stanley walked toward the door, pressed his ear to the door, and listened. In the hall Florence was saying:

"Mickey, you're a dear . . . an absolute dear. I'll take those things from you as soon as I find my key."

He could hear her fumbling.

"Oh, goodness, Mickey, you'll have to forgive me, sweetie. I don't seem to have a bit of change on me."

The elevator man said, "That's all right, Mrs. Moss."

"But you worked so hard carrying those big old heavy bags for me. Why don't you come in a minute and wait while I find some change?"

"No, really, it's okay. I'm glad to do it . . . for *you*."

"Well, aren't you a doll! If there's anything I can do to return the favor, Mick, don't fail to call on me." She laughed tipsily, amused that her teasing had embarrassed him.

"Good night, Mrs. Moss," Mickey said.

"Good night, Mickey." She laughed again to herself. Her face was relaxed, gay. As she opened the door and saw Stanley her face froze.

"Where've you been?" Stanley said.

"I've been out. Where've *you* been?"

She walked past him, through the dining room, into the kitchen. He followed at her heels.

"I've been here, waiting for you. What's the big idea?"

"Oh, leave me alone!" She put the groceries on the kitchen table.

"What do you mean . . . leave you alone?" Stanley said. "I expected you'd be here at seven o'clock. I expected I'd be given my dinner tonight. Is there anything wrong in that? What do you think I am anyway?"

"Some time when you've got a few hours to spare, I'll tell you!"

"You've been drinking again."

"Thank you, Sam Spade."

"I called Charlie's. He told me you were there this evening . . . for a long time."

She removed her coat. She was wearing a tight sweater. "He did, eh? Well, it's nice to know who your friends are."

"Florence, what's the matter with you? What do you suppose men think of a woman dressed like that, sitting at a bar in the middle of the afternoon?"

"I *know* what they think . . . and it's a damn sight more interesting than what *you* think."

"Don't talk like that, Florence!"

"I'll talk any way I want."

"Haven't you any pride?"

"Not as much as I had when I married you. What good does it do me to sit around this dump in the after-

noon all dolled up? Do you ever tell me I look nice? Do
you ever show me a good time? A woman has a right to
things like that and if you can't give me what I want,
there's lots of guys who can!"

Stanley clenched his fists. "I'm sorry, Florence, but
sitting in a saloon isn't my idea of a good time."

"Oh, it isn't mine either, but what else is there? You
think I have any laughs sitting around here at night,
watching you mope around with your books and papers?
Where's the can-opener?"

"It's over there. I was going to make myself some
soup, but I went to Riker's. Florence, I . . . I'm sorry if
you're not happy with me, but you shouldn't associate
with the kind of people you meet in bars in the afternoon. You don't know what kind of men you're liable
to meet."

"Don't I?"

"No. And what was the idea of falling all over the
elevator boy?"

"Falling all over who?"

"You heard me. 'Mickey, you're a dear.' Calling an
elevator boy *sweetie*. It's disgraceful!"

"What's disgraceful about it? He was very nice. He
carried my groceries for me, and I didn't have any
change."

"But your *attitude* . . . I was listening and it made me
sick to my stomach! You know, Florence, you're a very
exciting woman. Some time you're going to get a little
too friendly with one of these elevator boys or delivery
men and you're going to be sorry."

"All right. Let that be our thought for the day. I'm a very exciting woman. Stanley, you know what *you* are? You're a square! A genuine, A-number-one, gilt-edged *square*. Get me the coffee." He took a can of coffee from a cupboard and handed it to her.

"Aw, Florence, I don't want to argue with you. Why don't you kiss me when I see you in the evening, like other wives do?"

"Cut it."

"What's the matter?"

"Nothing's the matter. I'm just not in a mood to be pawed, that's all."

"I hope you felt the same while you were sitting at the bar this afternoon."

"You've got a vicious mouth! Get me a drink!"

"Don't you think you've had enough already?"

"Get me a drink!"

"All right." He took a bottle and a glass from the cupboard.

"And stop making all those unfunny comments about what I do on my own time. Before I married you you were more than happy to stand in line and wait your turn, mister . . . don't forget it!"

"But you're my *wife* now!"

"Stop reminding me!" The front door buzzer rang. "I'll get it," Florence said. "Keep an eye on the stove."

She walked into the front room, drying her hands. When she opened the door a Western Union boy was standing in the hall.

"Mrs. Florence Moss? Sign here," the boy said.

"Wait a minute," Florence said. She walked away from the door and reached up to the top of a glass-front chest that stood in the hall. "Stanley, is that change purse still up here?"

The boy eyed her as she exposed part of her leg in reaching up. He whistled softly. She smiled at him over her shoulder, took down a small coin purse, and extracted a quarter which she handed to the boy.

"Thank *you,* ma'am."

She closed the door.

"Florence!" Stanley said. "*Must* you flirt with everything that wears pants?"

"Don't tell me you're getting jealous of Western Union boys?"

"It isn't that I'm jealous, Florence. It's just that . . . well, that's no way for a lady to act."

"Thanks for the compliment."

"Who's the wire from?"

"I think this is a scene from that new picture called *None of Your Business.*" She opened the envelope and read the message. "If you must know it's from Dick Kramer."

"I didn't know you'd been seeing him."

"I haven't been seeing him. He just says he'll be in town tonight or in the morning. Business trip or something."

"Does he want to see you?"

"Of course he wants to see me."

"Oh. Well, don't let me stand in your way."

"Look, stupid, Dick Kramer is a much older friend of

mine than even *you* are. He's a darling, and if he has time I intend to see him. There's no harm in that!"

"If he's such an old and good friend why didn't you marry him when you had the chance?"

"Oh, stop! That's all water over the dam."

"Florence, why must you think that every man in the world is your personal property? Sometimes I think you're sick. I actually do."

"I am. Sick of you. Did you get the papers?"

"No. Why?"

"Give me some change. I'll send Mickey for the *News* and *Mirror*."

He handed her some change from his pocket. She walked to the door and opened it. At the doorway she stopped, speaking back into the room. "Is there anything else we need? Any beer or anything? As long as Mickey . . ." She broke off. She was staring at the wall just to the right of the door.

"What's the matter?" Stanley said, his throat tightening.

"Who did this?" Florence said.

"Who did what?"

"It's disgraceful! Where's there a pencil with an eraser on it?" She found a pencil in her purse and began to erase something on the wallpaper. "What kind of dump is this getting to be, anyway?" she said. "People drawing on the walls."

"What are you talking about?"

"Come here and look at this! You'd think this was the

back of a barn someplace . . . the pictures people think they can get away drawing."

He walked out into the hall. There was a smudged obscene drawing on the wallpaper.

"What's this over here? This writing?"

"It says, '*Lord, help me. Please. Before it's too late. Johnny.*'"

"Was this here before?" Stanley said. "When you came in?"

"No. Or if it was . . . I didn't notice. Why?"

"Oh, nothing."

"Well, I'll rub it out with . . ."

"No, wait."

"What for?"

"I'd like to know who did this, wouldn't you?"

"Yes."

"You're sure it wasn't here when you came in?"

"I don't know. I don't think it was."

"I knew something like this would happen."

"What are you talking about? Some punky kid scribbles a picture on the wallpaper. What do you mean you knew something like this would happen?"

"Florence, a *kid* might scribble something dirty on a wall, but this writing . . ."

"What about it?"

"Only a psychopath would write something like that!"

"What are you talking about? It says, '*Lord, help me. Please. Before it's too late. Johnny.*' I don't even know what it means."

"I don't either. But it sounds kind of familiar."

"You've seen it before?"

"No. I read something. I can't seem to . . . that case in Chicago a few years ago. Remember? There was this guy who would scribble a message on a wall or on a mirror every time he'd kill a woman."

"You trying to frighten me?"

"Don't be ridiculous. I don't like the looks of this. We'd better call the police."

They walked into the apartment and closed the door.

"No, wait. This is silly. You can't call the police just because somebody scribbles on your walls."

"You don't seem to get the point, Florence. We can erase what's on the wallpaper. That doesn't matter. What does worry me is that some unbalanced character . . . for all we know, a potential murderer . . . has been lurking out here in our hallway. Is there any writing anywhere else in the hall?"

They both walked out into the hall again and looked about.

"No. It just seems to be in this one place."

"Maybe we can handle this ourselves. Is there anyone who works in the building named Johnny?"

"Yes," Florence said.

"Who?"

"The night man. But it couldn't be him. He's a thousand years old."

"I guess you're right. Has anyone delivered anything here today? Did anything come from the delicatessen

this morning? Anything from a department store?"
Stanley was enjoying himself.

"No. Yesterday there was something. A man checking the light and gas meters."

"If only you could remember whether or not this scribbling was here when you came in a while ago. If it wasn't . . ."

"Then it must have been—oh, no. Not Mickey. His name's Mickey. Not Johnny!"

"I knew something like this was going to happen, Florence. You and your tight skirts and your sweaters . . . I warned you!"

"Shut up! This is no time for I-told-you-so speeches. You're supposed to be so smart. Do something. Figure this out!"

"I don't see how it could have been Mickey either. Although a man would hardly sign his own name to a thing like this. It could have been the boy with the telegram. Looks like whoever wrote it was fairly tall."

"That's right."

"See. I'm only five-seven, and if a tall man did the writing it would be up here like it is. What did the boy look like?"

"How do I know?"

"You certainly were friendly enough with him."

"Oh, stop. Look, why don't I just ring the buzzer and call Mickey and ask him if——"

"No, that's no good. If he did it he'll just deny it . . . then we'll never know. I still think I ought to call the police. Maybe they could check for fingerprints."

"Maybe. Maybe it could be one of the maintenance men."

"Maybe. Are any of them tall?"

"One of them is. But I've never spoken to any of them. They don't know me."

"I doubt that. What did the man who checked the meters look like?"

"He was cute. I mean he was . . . oh, I don't know. What difference does it make what he looked like?"

"What I want to know is, did he look odd in any way? Did he act suspicious? Did you flirt with him?"

"I gave him a cup of coffee. We talked for a minute. You call that flirting?"

"When the woman is you, yes!"

They walked back into the living room and closed the door.

"Well, I hope you're satisfied," Stanley said. "It could have been the meter man or Mickey or the doorman or the Western Union boy or even Dick Kramer."

"Oh, now you're being asinine."

"It's possible. Maybe he just sent the wire as a gag. He could already be in town. I never did trust him anyway."

"He wouldn't do a thing like this. He was a little wild, I'll admit, but not like this."

"Didn't you split up with him because of some trouble he got into about a girl?"

"Yes. I'd forgotten about that. But it couldn't be. Unless it's a prank. Only this isn't very funny."

The door buzzer grated harshly. Florence and Stanley stood rooted, looking at each other. The buzzer sounded again.

"Don't answer it," Florence whispered.

"No, wait. I'll tell you what. You answer it and I'll stand right behind the door. You'll be perfectly safe. I just want to get a line on who it is."

"I'm afraid."

"You're perfectly safe. I'll be right here. If *I* answer the door, I may frighten them away. If it's our man he might give himself away, if *you* answer."

A knock was heard at the door. Florence, ashen, advanced toward it.

"Who's there?"

The Western Union boy said something muffled behind the door.

"Go ahead. Open it," Stanley whispered.

The door opened.

"Another telegram, lady. Sign here."

"Thank you."

"Looks like you're pretty popular tonight. Here, you want to use my pencil?"

Stanley stepped out from behind the door. "I'll take that."

"Hey, what's the idea?" the boy said.

"You the boy who was here a few minutes ago?" Stanley said.

"Yeah. What's the matter . . . you want your tip back?"

Stanley stepped out into the hall. "I just want to see something." With the boy's pencil Stanley scribbled briefly on the wall.

"Mac, you're signing in the wrong place."

"Very funny, son. Did you do this writing on the wall?"

"What?"

Stanley said to Florence, "It looks like the same kind of lead . . . I can't tell for sure. Your name is Johnny, isn't it?"

"I don't know what you're talking about," the boy said. "My name is Wilbur."

"Somebody drew a dirty picture on the wall here! And somebody wrote something. See it? Did you do it? Did you?"

"Stanley, take it easy," Florence said.

"Lady, what's this guy talking about? If you two won't sign for that wire, it's nothing to me. I'm gettin' outta here." He retreated to the elevator door.

"All right. Get out! And don't come back. And don't act so friendly with this lady next time . . . you hear?"

Stanley and Florence walked back into the living room.

"There's no sense acting like that. You had no reason to frighten the kid like that."

"Why not? He frightened *you*, didn't he?"

"But you had nothing to go on. He didn't seem like the type."

"No. Who *is* the type? Who is the type, Florence? The type to get funny ideas about you into his head?

The type to follow you home and scribble nasty things on the wall outside your apartment? Tell me that if you wouldn't mind? Who is the type?"

"Ah, shut up. The way you're making a federal case out of this we'll never find out who we're looking for!"

"Florence, I love you."

"What?"

"Don't look at me as if I just said something shocking. Maybe you don't care . . . but I love you. And *because* I love you I worry about you. I'm trying to protect you, to take care of you."

"Stanley . . . you're jealous."

"Don't read lines at me, Florence. Of course I'm jealous."

"Why, baby," she said, "I never realized you had it in you. You're jealous as hell."

He tried to kiss her. She accepted a kiss on the cheek. "What's the idea? Don't you like the way your husband kisses?"

"Ah, shut up!"

Stanley was shouting now. "You have no right to talk to me like that. Don't do it again or you'll be sorry!"

There was a knock at the door. Stanley and Florence stood motionless. It was Mickey, the elevator man. "Mrs. Moss! Mrs. Moss!" He knocked again.

"Don't move," Stanley said. He walked to the door and opened it. "What do you want?"

"Oh, hello, Mr. Moss. I—uh——"

"You thought my wife was here alone?"

"No. I knew you were here. I could hear you yelling

out in the hall. I just came up to . . . I mean . . . well, the Western Union kid who was just here, he said he thought there was something wrong . . . so I—I just got off the elevator to check and I heard you yelling, that's all."

"Well, Mrs. Moss and I are very grateful to you, but there's nothing the matter."

"Well, that's fine. I just wanted to be helpful, that's all. Didn't want to cause any trouble. You know, if there was something wrong . . . I just wanted to be Johnny-on-the-spot."

"Mickey," Stanley said, "how did this scribbling get on the wall?"

"Where? Oh. I don't know. I'll send somebody up to clean it up right away."

"Don't bother. Before we have it cleaned off I think we'll have the police look at it."

"Oh, I wouldn't do that. Probably just some punky delivery boy or something with a new pencil. No sense gettin' anybody in trouble over a little thing like that."

"All right, Mickey. Thank you." Stanley closed the door.

"I can't believe it was him," Florence said.

"Why not? You know you appeal to him. You remember, of course, not fifteen minutes ago you were out in the hall practically flirting with him . . . deliberately asking for trouble!"

"You stop that crap!"

"You slut!"

"Watch it, Stanley. Watch it with the name-calling. I don't like it!"

"Don't you realize, Florence, that these men whose emotions you play around with are made of flesh and blood, just like I am? Don't you realize that if you give one of them the come-on he's liable to react in an unusual way. They know you're a married woman; they know they can't step into your life; so don't you realize that a thing like this is the most natural result in the world of—of what you've been doing?"

"I haven't been doing anything!"

"Stop lying! Stop lying in your teeth when I know you're lying. I know where you spend your afternoons. I know what you think of me. And now, a thing like this. It's more than a man can stand, Florence!"

"Who's asking you to stand it? Why don't you just shut up and leave me alone? If you want to accomplish something to show me what a big strong man you are, then go out and find out what bum did that scribbling. Don't just stand here and shout at me . . . what is *that?*"

"Don't try to order me around, Florence. I'll find out who did that scribbling. Don't worry about that. I'll find out and you'll find out, too. They say once a man does a thing like that he'll do it again. The urge will come over him again, Florence, if it has once already . . . don't worry about that. He'll show his face again."

"So all right. So fine! But in the meantime, stop talking to me like I was an idiot. I don't have to take your abuse!"

"Oh, yes you do. You're my wife, so I own you. And I'm very jealous of you and I don't like the idea that other men can joke with you and flirt with you and for all I know make love to you when you don't like to have me touch you. Not that I ever really want to, of course."

"I've heard about enough of that!"

"No, this is once you're not going to shut me up, Florence. Because you're afraid now. And the reason you're afraid is because there's somebody out there who may be able to do you harm, so you need me, you see? You need me. So you can't shut me up. You've brought this about yourself, you see? There's no one else to blame. I'm your husband and I've got a right to talk to you this way." His voice was high, ringing.

"Stanley, stop. That's enough!"

"No, it's not nearly enough. I should have done this a long time ago. I won you once. I never have been able to understand why I've had to win you time and time again, but now I understand. That's what you want. You don't want weakness. You admire strength. You despised me for being a gentleman and you sat with bums in saloons. Well, have it your way, Florence. You'll submit to me now. I want you."

"Take your lousy hands offa me," Florence shrieked. "You hear? Take your lousy fag hands offa me!" She started to say something about his having hands like his mother's and that was when he hit her.

He hit her first with the flat of his left hand and then punched her in the side of the head with his right. She kicked him in the shins and then he killed her with a large bread knife that he had bought at Macy's at a discount.

Somebody heard the fight and called the police. When they came Stanley was standing quietly in the hall, weeping, scribbling something on the wallpaper.

7

THE SIDEWALK

When I came around the corner at Fifty-fourth Street I saw Seventy on his hands and knees. His face was screwed up in concentration and his nose was close to the sidewalk.

"Hi," I said.

"Hi," he said. "Careful. Don't walk here where it's wet."

"Why not?" I said. He dipped a small brush into a glass of soapy water and brushed vigorously at the pavement. Half of one square of concrete was brushed clean.

"I'm trying to get the sidewalk clean," he answered.

"What for?"

"Oh, it's a long story," he said, "but I gotta get it all

clean. I figure this soap'll do the trick, then I can hose it down to wash the soap off."

"What's the idea?" I said.

"It's a long story."

I reached into the pocket of my jacket and took out a small, dark red rubber ball. While he brushed the sidewalk I stood there throwing the ball against the small space between two windows of the apartment house that stretched from the alley to the corner.

"Careful," Seventy said, "don't walk here where it's wet."

"Who's walking?" I said.

"I didn't say you were," Seventy said. "I just said be careful."

"All right," I said, "but what the hell's the big idea? You gonna clean up the whole city?"

"No," he said, "just this one square here." The square of cement bounded east and west by two cracks and north and south by the curb and a sparse lawn was now almost wholly moistened, cleaned by Seventy's brush.

"Al ain't home yet," Seventy said. "Go in the alley and find a tin can or a milk bottle."

"What for?"

"If Al ain't home I can't borrow his hose, so I'll need a tin can or something for the water."

"What water?"

"Judas, you're a dumb bastard. The water to wash all the soap off, what water do you think?"

"Oh," I said, frowning. I walked down the street a few steps and turned into the alley. Halfway down its length I found a milk bottle. When I brought it to him he walked across the grass and filled the bottle from the pipe that jutted from the brick wall. Then he shook it to clean the inside of the bottle, emptied the water on the grass, and refilled the bottle.

"This should do it," he said, splashing the water down hard on the pavement. The fluid scooped up tiny soap bubbles and cleaned little patches where soap had dried to a powdery film. Six times he filled the milk bottle and emptied its contents on the sidewalk. At last, satisfied with its cleanliness, he sat down on the curb in his faded brown corduroys and unbuttoned his collar.

"Now what?" I said.

"Now we're all set," he said.

"All set for what?" I asked. He looked at me the way people look at a dog that just isn't learning the simplest of tricks.

"Judas, you're a dumb bastard," he said, "but I guess I'll have to lay it all out for you. I just cleaned me off a nice little stretch of sidewalk here."

"Thanks a lot," I said, with all the sarcasm I could muster. "I thought maybe you were playing baseball or something." This struck me as a crushingly clever retort.

"Tell you what," Seventy said. "Maybe you can help me out. You got a quarter?"

"Yeah. I've got thirty-five cents. Why?"

"Why do you think," Seventy said. "Because I want to borrow it, that's why." I gave him the quarter and he said, "If this little deal comes off I'll give you back fifty cents for your quarter. Okay?"

"Okay," I said. "What do we do now?"

"Head for the Bluebird Diner," he said, standing up and dusting off his pants. At the Bluebird he carefully examined the menu as I drained both glasses of water the counter man had set before us.

"What'll it be?" the counter man asked tiredly.

"The chicken à la king should do it," Seventy told him.

"You want it on the dinner?" the man said.

"No," Seventy said. "To go. And just the chicken à la king in a carton or something. Nothing else."

The man looked at me. "You want anything?" he said.

"No," I said. "I'm with him." Walking back to Fifty-fourth I lovingly fingered the warm paper bag and the carton inside it. I could feel the heat from the creamy chicken warming my cold fingers.

"The sidewalk should be dried off by now," Seventy said.

"I guess you're right," I said, as we rounded the corner. I could see that the film of water had disappeared and the square of pavement Seventy had so diligently cleaned gave no immediate evidence of having been so recently scoured.

"Well," he said, squinting his eyes and pursing his lips, "I guess we're just about all set." I started to say "For what?" but checked myself. Seventy hated to be prodded and I refused to lower myself by any further demonstrations of insatiable curiosity.

"One thing, though," he added. "We'll have to figure out some way to keep people from walking on it."

100

"Walking on what?" I said, without thinking, then bit my lip.

"Tell you what," he said, not pressing his advantage, "let's pull that horse over here." He referred to a yellow wooden sawhorse flanked by two oil lanterns that the city had left in the street to warn motorists of the presence of an unusually deep depression in the asphalt.

"Isn't that liable to cause trouble?" I asked.

"No," he said. "The two red lanterns will guard the bump and besides we can put the thing back later."

When we had carried the guard horse to the curb and slanted it diagonally across the washed square of pavement Seventy picked up the bag of chicken à la king, deftly opened the carton, and without a word splattered its contents down on the sidewalk.

"You crazy?" I asked.

"When are you gonna stop asking stupid questions?" he said. "What time is it?"

"I don't know. It was about half-past five when we left the Bluebird."

"Okay, then it's about time Nick should be gettin' home from work. Let's go down to Woodlawn 'cause I gotta get the bread before he gets off the bus."

By this time I was so angry I wouldn't have asked another question if my life had depended on it. When we got to Woodlawn Avenue we went down the street to the A.&P. and bought a loaf of bread, sliced. Seventy made sure it was sliced. Without talking we hurried out of the A.&P. and walked up to Fifty-third Street.

"Let's not stand right here on the corner," Seventy

said. "Let's wait down here by the shoe store, so's it'll look like we were just passing by."

I didn't say anything. We waited near the shoe store and in about five minutes the bus stopped near the corner. Seventy hurried toward it and then slowed down and sauntered past the drugstore just as Nick was getting off the bus.

"Let on you don't see him," Seventy whispered. We turned the corner and walked on ahead of Nick, listening to his cleated heels clicking on the pavement behind us. Nick always wore cleats on the heels of his shiny, pointed shoes. Nick was a pretty sharp operator.

His full name was Nick Depopolous and around the neighborhood he liked to be referred to as Nick, the Greek, which he was. I think he had read something in a magazine once about the well-known gambler, Nick the Greek, and had selected the man as a personal idol. Nick needn't have patterned himself after anybody. He was tall, well-built, good-looking in a sort of George Raft-ish way, a natty dresser, and popular with the girls. He worked downtown as a shipping clerk, but he spent a lot of time around the Green Mill Poolroom on Fifty-fifth Street and he liked to gamble. Nick would take a bet on anything, and though he rarely wagered more than ten or fifteen dollars at a time, this made him a big gambler in the eyes of most of the kids in the neighborhood.

"Hi, Seventy." Nick had come abreast of us. Seventy's face lit up. He could not have acted more surprised if the King of England had come up behind us.

"Why, Nick," he said, "I haven't seen you in a week or so. Where've you been keeping yourself?"

"Oh, here and there," Nick said. "What's new with you guys?"

"Nothing much," I said.

We walked on for a few feet in silence, then Seventy said, "How the ponies treating you, Nick?"

"Fair enough," Nick answered. "Almost had a daily double this afternoon." Nick was only eighteen but to me he seemed a man of the world.

"This guy'll kill you," Seventy said to me. "Bets on anything. Nick, tell him about the time you bet Al Dietz he didn't know what color socks he was wearing."

"Sucker bet," Nick said modestly. "Nothing to it."

Seventy laughed in vast admiration. "Get him," he said. "Nothing to it. How about the time you bet old man Walters ten bucks his cigarette lighter wouldn't light the first time he tried it?"

"Sucker bet," Nick said, thrusting his lower lip out with slight pride.

Seventy laughed again. "I'm tellin' ya, there's nothing this guy won't bet on. Funny part of it is, he usually wins."

"No kidding?" I said.

"That's right," Seventy said as we turned the corner.

"Why, I saw him one time when he bet Bob Petrolli that he could swallow a live goldfish. Did it, too. Didn't ya, Nick?"

"Yep," Nick admitted. "If the price is right, I guess a guy'll do just about anything."

"Yessirree," Seventy said. "That's the way I feel about it, too. A guy might think he couldn't eat a gold-fish, but you put a sawbuck on the line and there's a lot of guys would try it. Right, Nick?"

"Right you are," Nick said. "Of course, the price has to be right."

"And the guy has to have guts, too," Seventy said.

"Oh, of course," Nick agreed. "If you ain't got guts, you got no right to make a bet in the first place."

"I got just as much guts as you have, Nick, only I don't seem to have the money to back it up," Seventy said, with sudden abandon. A flicker of surprise at his tone crossed Nick's face. We had almost walked up to the cleaned square of pavement, the spilled chicken à la king that lay splashed on the pavement, and the saw-horse that partially blocked the path.

"So you got guts," Nick said.

"You're darned right," Seventy said. "Eating live goldfish!" He sneered. "Why, if somebody was to make me the right kind of a bet I'd even eat *that*." He pointed with a rigid finger at the cold, creamy mess that he had thrown on the sidewalk.

I was looking at Nick. When he saw what Seventy was pointing at, his face screwed up with displeasure and he turned his eyes away, stepping gingerly across the splat-tered area. I held my breath. Nick walked on a few feet, then halted and turned around. He looked at Seventy.

"What did you say?" he asked.

"I said that if somebody made me the right kind of a bet, I'd even eat that!" He pointed again, but Nick's eyes refused to lower. They were momentarily expressionless, then a methodical glint came into them. Nick slanted his head to one side and regarded Seventy with a superior smile.

"You talk big," he said. "I got twenty-five dollars I'll put up against your five that says you can't do no such thing. That is," he smiled with even more contempt, "if you can raise five bucks."

"Don't you worry about me," Seventy said. There was a pause.

"Well, big boy," Nick said. "How about it? We got a bet or have you chickened out already?" Seventy hesitated. I couldn't help admiring his timing.

"That's what I thought," Nick said. "You punks around here talk pretty big, but when it comes to putting up you ain't got what it takes."

"That does it," Seventy said. "You got a bet!"

"Okay," Nick said. "So I got a bet. But it don't look to me as if I'm gonna lose it. As a matter of fact," he said, "I'll do you a favor. You can welsh out right now and we'll call the whole thing off."

Seventy didn't answer. Instead he opened the wax paper wrapped on the bread he was carrying and took out one slice. Tearing it in half, he solemnly got down on his knees and carefully sopped up a large gob of chicken à la king from the spotless pavement. Nick's eyes almost popped out of his head.

"Holy God!" he said.

Expressionlessly Seventy lifted the slice of bread to his mouth, bit off a large piece, and wiped more chicken from the sidewalk with the rest of the slice, then put it into his mouth, closed his eyes tight as if suffering great pain, and wolfed the bread and chicken down.

Nick was pale now. Through tight lips he gasped, "That's enough. Cut it out!" With trembling fingers he withdrew his wallet from a back pocket, produced two tens and a five, and handed them to Seventy, then without a word he turned and hurried away, groaning slightly.

Seventy and I went back to the A.&P., got five ones for the five, and Seventy handed me one of the bills.

He came by that nickname because even though he was only fifteen he had the wisdom of an old man. I haven't seen him in years now, but I guess he's doing all right.

8

THE STRANGERS

We are all shocked and made unhappy if we see a jackal devour a rabbit, yet at this moment white teeth are sinking into furtive fur and tearing panicked flesh in all the jungles of the world and we are unaffected by the knowledge.

We wince if we hear that in the saloon on the next block a man was cut with a knife, but across the world men are daily cut to pieces and we are unmoved. Distance lends unreality.

We teach that our mothers and fathers must be honored and we honor them not. We are accustomed to coveting our neighbors' goods and our neighbors' wives. We are not even certain which day *is* the Sabbath day, hence we have difficulty keeping it holy. We find it, ordinarily, impossible to fall in love with God. All of us make something of a habit of bearing false witness against our neighbor. One of the rare occasions on which we will not bear false witness against him is when we are able to broadcast some damaging truth about him.

Those of us who do not commit adultery are almost without exception those who have not the opportunity. The rest are merely those who have not the inclination.

We say it is wrong to kill, but we kill cockroaches and pigs and hamsters and daffodils and burglars and Jews and Negroes and intruders and time and initiative and joy or anything that is convenient for us to kill.

Two of us pulled into a gas station outside of Indio, California, one day in late summer. It was about two days after Dan Scanlon had left New York.

The two were Mormons: Homer Snow and his wife Betsy. They had been visiting with Betsy's relatives in San Diego for three weeks and now they were driving back across the desert on their way to their home in Provo, Utah.

Homer was a bishop of his church but he was also a dentist. The title *bishop* does not mean quite the same thing to the Church of Jesus Christ of the Latter-day Saints that it means to the other churches of Christendom, so it was not unusual that Homer wore no ecclesiastical robes and that he pulled teeth and also sold a little insurance on the side.

The Mormons are a thrifty and respectable people and Homer had saved a considerable amount of money during the twenty-four years he had been married to Betsy. He owned the two-story building in Provo in which he had set up his professional offices, and since his time was largely his own he was able each year to take a month's vacation.

He was as rangily tall and easygoing as his wife was small and shrewish. And yet, for all his good nature and for all her calculating determination, Homer was the boss and Betsy meekly did his bidding.

They had raised four children, put them through high school and college, and seen them all happily married. One of the girls had taken a job in Dallas and married a semi-Baptist and fallen away from the church, but this was the only black mark on the Snow's religious record.

They were well liked in Provo and though they had accumulated some riches and learned a fair amount about the rest of the world, they clung tenaciously to their faith and observed all its admonitions and restrictions. They did not drink coffee, tea, or Coca-Cola and Betsy had never tasted liquor of any kind, although once in a great while if Homer happened to be out of town alone and among strangers he would take a drink.

They had a large radio in their front room and they subscribed to *Time, Collier's,* and *Reader's Digest,* yet they still believed that Christ would return in bodily form to the earth during their lifetime.

During the war they had stored away vast quantities of canned peaches, pears, Spam, Florida orange juice, flour (in glass jars), blackberry jam, peas, baked beans, applesauce, soups, and pineapple, for the church had passed along the word that a famine might soon fall upon the land and that the Saints would therefore do well to provide themselves with as many of the edible necessities as they thought would store well without spoiling. There was some embarrassment among the faithful when Washington let it be known that to hoard was unpatriotic; but by simply not thinking about the conflict of interests, very often most of the Saints were able to go about their business and do whatever else they could to help the war effort.

Homer got along quite well with the non-Mormon members of his community, although he could not abide the Catholics because of their conceit and their belief that they were the one, true fold.

Of all the non-Mormons he had met and discussed religion with, only the Catholics seemed to have a faith as strong as his own. He attributed their success and their alarming increase to the direct help of Satan, although he often thanked God that Utah was still largely a Mormon state. He was alarmed about the problem of communism but he was secretly pleased about the war between Moscow and Rome. He considered that it was the will of God that two such powerful forces for evil should expend so much of their energy against each other.

Stopped now outside of Indio, he hooked the scratched bronze nozzle of a water hose over the mouth of the open radiator of his 1951 Dodge. A faint wisp of steam issued from the open pipe, and as he leaned over to look down its length the smell of hot oil assailed his nostrils.

"Help you?" said the station attendant.

"Yes," Homer said. "Give me five regular."

The attendant moved around to the back of the car as Homer sprayed the honeycombed radiator front with water to wash away the bugs and cool off the motor.

"Want to get out and stretch your legs?" he said to Betsy.

"No," she said, "I'm all right." Scattered bits of hair stuck wetly to the back of her neck and she fanned vaguely at her chest with a limp handkerchief, but Homer had known that she would not get out of the car and go into the station to keep cool. Betsy enjoyed being a martyr, and Homer was so used to her attitude by now that he would have been emotionally jarred if she had suddenly changed. She had sacrificed much to raise her children, had learned to sew exceptionally well to save money on clothing, and had seen to it that the children had had many of the "advantages" that she had been denied. It never occurred to her that, now that the children were out on their own and she and Homer had more than enough money, she no longer had any need to deny herself.

She wore no make-up, she had never owned a fur coat, she mended her own stockings, and she had never taken a penny from any of the children.

She sat primly, looking out at the dry desert foliage and the empty, hot sky. Homer had lowered the hood of the car and she could look straight ahead again. Heat waves wrinkled and waved the objects that she regarded, lizardlike, through the windshield, and after a few moments her eyelids became heavy and she dozed slightly sitting there in her mussed lavender cotton-print dress.

She had not slept well the night before in the motel in Pasadena. She had wanted to stay at a hotel, but Homer had preferred the convenience and the savings that a motor-court stop represented.

All night long cars had whispered by on the highway outside. She had lain in the twin bed by the window, tossing and turning and muttering, "Goodness," and "Land."

She finally had fallen asleep shortly after midnight and thereafter awakened fully only twice, but when she had gotten up in the morning she had groaned and said, "I didn't sleep a wink. Not one wink."

"You snored," Homer said.

"I did not," she said, walking into the too-small bathroom.

Lying in his underwear in the unfamiliar bed, listening to her washing her face and flushing the toilet, Homer had known a flicker of desire and had felt himself briefly. Sitting on the side of the bed he thought for a moment of Sarah, his receptionist, for it had been at least ten years since he had actively desired his wife, and though Sarah was married he still could not keep himself from looking at her sometimes as she moved efficiently about the office.

Fortunately for his peace of mind, desire came upon him very rarely. He stood now, scratching his stomach and yawning and said, "It's only eight-thirty. I thought it was later."

"Time we were on our way," Betsy said.

"Remind me to pick up some postcards for Davey later, will you?"

"Yes. We can get them when we stop for breakfast."

Homer had little use for Betsy's people in San Diego but he loved his nephew, Davey Udall. Davey was five years old and blond and affectionate, and Homer made it a point to send him a little postcard message now and then. In San Diego or "Dago," as Homer rakishly learned to call it, he would take Davey for long rides or for walks along the waterfront. They would stop and talk to men fishing and Homer would buy Davey ice-cream cones and tell him stories about Utah.

Pulling out of the gas station, he kept the car in second gear.

"Why are you driving so slowly?" Betsy said.

"Looking for a place to buy postcards," Homer said.

He saw another gas station joined to a grocery and novelty store and pulled the car off the highway and up into the shaded gravel near the building.

In a moment he was back in the car, smiling.

"Got some nice ones," he said. "One with a little Indian boy riding a jackass."

"That's nice," Betsy said.

They drove along the highway at slightly more than sixty miles an hour, not speaking. Occasionally a car would whip past them, edging Homer over to the right a bit, and he would shake his head and say, "Crazy fool," or "I hope he gets there on time."

That night they stopped in Phoenix at the home of

Homer's brother, Joe. Joe was older than Homer by four years, and he ran a used-car lot.

"Why don't you folks stay over a few more days?" Joe said the next morning, standing on his front lawn, leaning against their car.

"Oh, you know," Homer said. "Betsy's anxious to get back and everything. We'd like to, but I'm afraid we'll have to wait till next time around."

They had an appointment anyway.

"Well, take care of yourselves," Joe said, backing off and waving, stooped-over, as Homer gunned the motor gently.

"You, too," Betsy said, waving a loose hand.

"Write," Joe said.

"You bet," Homer called back.

There were mirages before Homer on the highway now as he sped north out of Phoenix. Dips in the road ahead appeared to be full of water and the numbing heat of the desert pressed down upon the car, made the motor run hot, and dried the throats of Homer and Betsy.

They felt sleepy and Homer turned on the radio. He tried to find a newscast but there seemed to be nothing on but cowboy or jazz music and interminable commercials. Betsy flicked a button and silence filled the car, broken only by the steady hum of the tires on the hot pavement.

"Just a little love," sang Homer, "a little kiss. I would give you all my life for this . . ."

Shortly thereafter, about the time Homer ran over a

rabbit, Dan was turning off Highway 66 and pushing his car steadily toward Phoenix. He had been on the road for three days and he was nervous and jumpy.

The first night out of New York he had driven on the Pennsylvania Turnpike and got lost for over an hour trying to get out of Pittsburgh.

A stupid gas-station mechanic had given him the wrong directions just before an important junction, and he had found himself getting deeper and deeper into the Allegheny hills above Pittsburgh, on a narrow road that became more desolate with each passing mile.

Below him in the valleys strange flames glowed in the night and layers of blue smoke hung thickly over the landscape.

Irritably he screeched to a stop and shouted to a boy on a bicycle, "Is this the way to Wheeling?"

"No, *sir!*" the boy said, laughing.

"Goddammit," Dan shouted, whipping the car around. "Son-of-a-bitch!" He had driven at least twenty-five miles out of Pittsburgh and now, on the way back to town, traffic unaccountably piled up in front of him and he could not make time. He drove all night to make up for the delay and did not sleep until almost noon the next day.

When he woke up in the dingy motel in the small West Virginia town, he felt dizzy and sick to his stomach. A shave and shower picked him up, but he was disgusted to see that it was after six o'clock and already beginning to get dark.

He drove all night again, squinting at the lights of

oncoming cars, stopping now and then to drink a Coke or have a hamburger and coffee while the car was being filled with gasoline.

At first he had eaten good steaks and heavy desserts and tipped lavishly, but now as he stood under the dim neon-blue light of a tiny gas station in Missouri, counting his money, he was startled to observe that there were only thirty-nine dollars in his wallet.

He thereafter ate less expensive food and began taking peanuts and packaged cookies with him in the car and using regular instead of ethyl gasoline.

He stayed at the cheapest motels he could find and counted his money again and again and finally figured out that he had lost a twenty-dollar bill somewhere along the way.

Now and then he would pass hitchhikers standing like patient statues along the road or under lamp posts at lonely intersections. Some fear made him refuse to pick them up. It was strange. Now that he was a motorist, now that he had money (somewhere, if not in his pocket), now that he had a big car with a shiny exterior and a powerful motor, now that he rode like a baron unarmed in a strange forest, he was not inclined to stop or to think of how his speeding past affected the stolid, lonely people who stood with thumbs lifted by the side of the road.

He had possessions and he did not want to risk them. It was just one minor example, but it illustrated perfectly the difficulty of being truly Christian.

116

It was the same old thing: the truth and the exception. The ideal and the expediency.

He listened on the car radio to a disc jockey playing Stan Kenton records and passed lonely figures in the night.

He had been a hitchhiker once and had stood angrily in gutters and beside ditches. He could still remember the feeling, still recall vividly muttering threats and orders at passing cars. Hitchhikers, he thought, with their veiled shoutings and demands, were like poets who are forever standing on verbal hilltops with their shirts open, shouting instructions to the elements:

"Roll on, thou deep and dark blue ocean, roll!"

"Blow, blow, thou wintry wind!"

"Stop, you mother-grabber, stop for me!"

He saw himself clearly, standing by the highway in Arkansas (or had it been Texas?), when he had run away from home years before.

Standing by the side of the road, he alternately prayed and swore as car after car passed him by. Sometimes after half-a-hundred cars had gone by, tires whining on the pavement, he would make little efforts toward improving his appearance. People were afraid of hitchhikers. Perhaps he looked too dirty, too threatening. He removed his hat, folded it flat, and shoved it up under his sweater, along one side. Then he took out his broken comb and combed his hair. His handkerchief was wrinkled and filthy, but he rubbed it on his face to remove some of the dirt. There was a chill in the air and his jacket was zipped up tight under his chin, but it would be better, he thought, if it were open at the neck and neatly folded back at the collar to show a little of his shirt. With the zipper lowered a few inches the air lay cold on his neck, but he knew that he looked a little better, a little less threatening. Without the hat more of his face was visible and as cars approached now he smiled, tried to look innocent, harmless, friendly, casual.

A car was approaching and he slicked down his hair with one last pat, then moved out onto the road to make sure the driver could see him. He opened his eyes and smiled idiotically as he lifted his right hand. The car did not slow down.

The rush of air as the car hurtled past made his eyes water, and a sudden rush of anger forced the corners of his mouth down.

"Lousy son-of-a-bitch!" he said, looking at the disappearing rectangle that grew smaller far down the highway. "Lousy son-of-a-bitch!"

After a moment his anger subsided, but a feeling of sullen resentment remained. To hell with all the people with cars, the lousy, selfish bastards! It wouldn't cost any of them a cent to stop and give him a lift. No skin off their noses, the selfish bastards. He wished he had a gun. It would be great to give the next bastard that came along a good square chance to stop. Wave at him nice and friendly and show him the old thumb, and then if he didn't stop whip out the gun and blast the son-of-a-bitch off the road.

His mouth turned down again as he fancied himself pumping bullets into the back of a car, the back of the driver's head, seeing the vehicle careen and wobble off the road, seeing it turn over and burst into flame. The dirty, lousy bastards. It would serve them right. If he had a car he'd be glad to stop for them. Why wouldn't they show him the same courtesy? What the hell; they weren't any better than he was. Lousy hillbillies, they weren't as *good* as he was. Who the hell wanted to ride in their goddammed rattle-traps anyway? All he wanted was to get the hell out of that neck of the woods for good!

He zipped his jacket up tight under his chin again. Why the hell should he catch cold to please a bunch of stupid hillbillies?

He walked along for a while, disdaining to even turn and face the cars and continued to speed past him. For perhaps twenty minutes he stalked along, kicking at rusty beer cans and stones, muttering epithets.

The throaty, grinding rumble of a truck sounded behind him distantly and he turned, feeling hope again in the instant. Some truck drivers shrugged apologetically, pointing to the "No Riders" sign pasted on their windshields. They seemed like nice guys and it wasn't their fault if they weren't allowed by their companies to pick up hitchhikers. Others just didn't give you a tumble and they could go to hell. But a lot of them stopped. Truck drivers, mostly, were good guys. Maybe this one would stop.

He stepped out onto the road and lifted his hand, his

head cocked eagerly, his ears tuned to pick up the slightest change in the roar of the motor that might indicate that the truck was slackening speed. It seemed to be a giant Mack, he thought, as it loomed larger.

He peered intently at the cab, wavered, then condescended to wear the simpering smile again, trying to see the driver, establish contact, read his expression.

For a moment he could tell the man at the wheel had lifted his foot from the accelerator and then, miraculously, the juggernaut was slowing down. His heart leaped up and his smile was genuine as he trotted up to the side door. Two Negroes regarded him without expression through the open window.

"How far you goin'?" one of them said.

"As far as you are," he answered.

"Okay," said the driver. "You can ride in back." He trotted to the back of the truck and pulled himself up. The back was walled and deep like that of a coal truck, but when his eyes reached the level of the rim he saw it was piled high with what looked like dirty cotton.

As the driver gunned the motor tentatively, he flung himself over the tail of the truck and sank deep into the cloudy pile of fiber.

"Hey," he shouted at the men in the cab, clambering forward, "what is this stuff?"

"Cotton seed" shouted the man next to the driver. The rest of his words were drowned out by the grinding of the motor as the truck gathered speed again.

Riding in the back, he squirmed around till he was

spread-eagled, his face to the sky, luxuriating in the resilient softness of the load of fiber-stuck cotton seeds. The drone of the motor, the yellow-streaked, late-afternoon clouds, and the blue of the sky were all he could sense of the world as he stretched and lolled on his magic carpet. The air was still chilled but he did not care, snuggled in the cotton. He wished that he could ride thus forever and he felt guilty at the bitterness that had been in his heart. This was really beautiful country and from his royal vantage point he now surveyed the Southern sky and the tips and branches of trees with a warm and appreciative feeling. He drunkenly reveled in the comfort that had fallen his lot, turning over on his stomach, flexing his muscles, yawning loudly, rolling onto his back again to lose himself in the bare, limitless beauty of the sky. For perhaps a quarter of an hour he lay like a drunken oriental potentate till, literally overcome by comfort, he relaxed completely and slept.

Recalling the feeling of warmth now, he smiled sleepily and reflected with slight sadness over the passing of youth's ability to appreciate pleasure in its own peculiar, delicious, rawly sensitive way.

But still he did not pick up any hitchhikers. Perhaps it was just as well.

Coming through Oklahoma he was eating more peanuts, drinking more Cokes and chocolate milk, and eating less real food. The money problem now was acute. He considered stopping and wiring ahead to Helen for money, but that would have meant waiting for twelve or eighteen hours in some out-of-the-way spot while she answered him, and so at last he decided to gamble on making the money last.

That night he did not go to a motel at all but slept in the car, twisted stiffly on the front seat. Actually it was after dawn when he pulled off the road and stopped and curled up and went to sleep. When he awakened his mouth felt bone-dry and bitter.

He had had a dream about Elaine and as he began to clear the shrouds of sleep from his brain, he tried to remember what he had been dreaming about.

It had seemed that he had been walking with her by a body of water, perhaps an ocean. They had walked along, hand in hand, on broken, furrowed earth that fell away and sloped down sharply, among rocks, to the water line.

He had stepped out onto the rocks and then been terri-fied to see that the water was washing the dirt away from among them. He was at last left high and dry on one tall, thin columnar rock that teetered in unstable sections beneath him. Elaine was somewhere near and he recalled having tried to hold her to him, to put his arms around her, and to put his hands on her body, but then she had receded and he had been terror-stricken again at the precariousness of his position.

When he was fully awake the memory of the dream left him, although he was left with a quivering, early-morning desire for a woman.

He pulled himself up to a sitting position and sat

half dazed with his eyes closed, trying to pull himself together.

He looked at his wrist-watch and discovered that he had slept only a little over three hours. It was fully fifteen minutes before he could summon up enough energy to step out of the car and flex his muscles.

The morning air felt cool and refreshing on his face, and to stir up the blood in his head he rubbed his cheeks and chin vigorously with both hands, feeling the beard stubble sliding under his fingers.

His mouth was sour and he spat again and again and inhaled deeply to clear it out. With trembling fingers he took a package of gum out of his pants pockets and put two pieces in his mouth. The sugar was immediately sucked into his system and helped a little to wake him up more completely and the flavoring in the gum made him less displeased with his mouth.

Cars slipped by at long intervals in the cool morning air, and he waited for a few minutes till the horizon was clear on all sides, than stepped away from the car a short distance and urinated, shivering.

When he got back behind the wheel the car seemed hot and stuffy again, for the sun was well up in the sky and beginning to burn off the cold air that had accumulated on the desert during the night.

Half an hour later he stopped at a roadside market and bought a pound of juicy purple grapes for breakfast.

He also stopped for gas and washed his face with

cold water, and when he got back in the car he was whistling a little, although he was still very tired.

For three days he had tried not to think of what he would have to do when he got to Los Angeles. At times he would think of the prospect of marrying Elaine and settling things once and for all and he would feel excited and happy, but then after a few minutes he would begin to worry and wonder about what Helen would say and what the children's reactions might be and he began to wonder how he would break the news to his mother.

Then he would turn on the radio and try to become absorbed in a newscast or a soap opera.

Although he was hurrying to Elaine, things had not, it seemed, changed so much after all, and the knowledge saddened him.

He had left New York in a mood of some defiance and conviction, but he had not been able to sustain the bravado, and now he could pull it back only by fits and starts. Sometimes a simple physical longing for Helen would overcome him and he found that he was able to convert the feeling into a sort of strength, a sort of armor for the battle that he feared lay ahead.

"Perhaps," he said to himself, "when I get there Elaine will tell me she loves someone else. I'll feel bad for a while, but then maybe that will make everything all right and I can go back to Helen."

Then the squirrel cage would begin turning again, and pros and cons would tumble back and forth in his mind so rapidly that he could not get them into any sort of order at all.

But some of the time he had the idea in his mind that he was going out to Los Angeles to marry Elaine and he felt pretty good about the whole thing.

After all, Helen was happy with Randy. Maybe everything would be all right.

He began driving faster now on the road coming south toward Phoenix, although parts of the road were twisted and dangerous. His brain felt numb again and he began to get drowsy, but at each possible stop he would step down hard on the accelerator and say. "Just a little farther and then I'll pull up." For perhaps twenty-five miles he pushed himself past stop after stop, thinking each time that the next place would be more inviting. Once he found himself slowed to a crawl by two giant trailer-trucks that were held to a snail's pace by a slight incline in the highway.

He tried to pass them, but the road ahead was either curved or blocked by oncoming cars, so at last he settled down to the speed of the trucks and crept along behind them, frustrated and furious for several minutes.

Finally an opportunity opened up and he swept past the two juggernauts and resumed his former high speed.

The road wound its way into mountainous country now and he was glad, for the flat land made for monotonous driving. He blinked to clear his head and rest his eyes and began holding the steering wheel more firmly as fatigue assailed him again.

Shortly after noon he began talking to himself and said, "Go just fifteen more minutes and then stop at the very next place you come to. You have to stop and go to the toilet, rest, and have something else to eat."

He nodded, by way of agreeing with his decision, and began going just a bit faster so as to squeeze the last possible mile out of the time limit he had set for himself.

The speedometer needle now showed that he was traveling between seventy and eighty miles an hour, although he did not realize he was going that fast. The car handled beautifully and hugged the road well on the long, gradual curves that unfolded before him through the mountains.

The scenery was striking, although because of his fatigue he appreciated it only rather dimly. The sky was desert-blue, cloudless, and hot, and the mountains were clearly etched in great, jagged, purplish masses against its background. Close by the road stately saguaros loomed out of the desert floor, and a million heavy rocks lay baking at the foot of the mountains from the surfaces of which they had been wrested by time and gravity.

The vistas were so far-reaching, the distances over which the eye could sweep so vast, that it seemed to Dan, when he looked away from the road, that he was crawling at a pallbearer's pace and would never cover the long, wild, empty stretch to the next mountain range.

In the mountains now there was much static on the radio and he finally could not stand to listen to it.

In Los Angeles at that moment Helen was bathing the baby, kneeling beside the tub in the front bathroom, saying, "That's it, sweetheart. Close your eyes while Mama gets the soap off your face and then we'll have a niiiccee nap, won't we?"

Randy was at a Safeway store, shopping for the week's groceries, and Michael and Patrick were with him, helping to push the wheeled basket down the aisles, asking him to buy Wheaties so they could send in the box top with a quarter and get a magic-code ring.

In Beverly Hills Elaine was having lunch with her mother, sitting in the kitchen, wearing a slightly soiled pink housecoat, saying, "Who called early this morning?"

"I think it was Jack whatshisname," her mother said. "He said he was only going to be in town for two days. I told him you'd call back. He's at the Ambassador."

"Thanks," Elaine said, pouring herself a second cup of coffee.

Dan was holding the car steadily on the road now, his mind numbly calm, almost happy. He was wondering if the next stop would be a good place to eat. The fifteen-minute period was almost over.

He shook his head once to throw the dark specter of sleep out of his brain, and then began squinting carefully, trying to drive with his eyes half closed and his head tilted back so that he could see the road quite clearly under the lids. He felt warm and relaxed. As he was coming up out of a slight dip in the road his head nodded, forced down as the car climbed the incline out of the dip, and it was then that the other car bore down upon him. He did not know that he was driving in the center of the road, straddling the white line, and he was never to know it.

His speed did not slacken, but the driver of the other

car jammed down violently on his brakes and grabbed the steering wheel hard when he saw Dan's Buick dead ahead.

The other car started to pull away to its right, but it was too late to help; the autos hit together, not exactly head on, for the other car had angled itself a little to one side, but with tremendous force nevertheless.

The top of Dan's head hit the windshield squarely and his chest was pushed back against the seat, driven back by the steering wheel which buckled in his hands and lifted his legs up off the floorboard, breaking them.

The man in the other car was thrown against his windshield at a slight angle and his steering wheel hit him a glancing blow, breaking his arms. The woman beside him was dashed into the windshield as forcibly as if she had been shot out of a cannon. She died in the instant.

Lizards and rabbits and buzzards scuttled in terror among the hills as the deafening roar of the impact echoed across the desert floor and bounced back off the mountain walls.

The Buick stopped almost squarely where it had been hit, twisted halfway around so that it was facing off the side of the road; the other car rolled over three times and came to rest among the cactus and tumbleweed that edged the highway. It lay on its right side a full thirty-five yards from the Buick, and when steam stopped pouring from its radiator an ominous silence fell over the scene, broken only by the soft whipping of the wind as it slipped among the desert brush.

Three minutes later a Pontiac with Michigan license plates stopped and a man got out and looked first at the Buick and then at the other car.

He walked fearfully over to the Buick and looked in.

"Holy God," he said and then broke into a run and got back in his car and raced off at high speed. Not far down the road he skidded to a stop at a gas station. Leaving the door of his car open, he ran into the station, knocking down a little girl who was playing by the door.

"I'm sorry, sweetheart," he said, picking her up. "Listen, is there a phone here?"

"Yes," said a tanned elderly man with short-cropped white hair. "What's the matter?"

"There's been an accident. An awful one. Right back up the road. You better get help, quick."

"Lord, God," said the elderly man, stepping out quickly from behind a counter, "that's the second one this month."

He took the phone off the hook and spoke loudly into the mouthpiece when he had gotten an operator on the line.

"Get the highway police, quick," he said. "Another accident up the road here. Yeah, this is Charley. Tell 'em where, will you? Wait a minute." He turned to the man at the door. "Where was it? North or south of here? I didn't notice which way you drove up."

"Up that way," said the man, pointing. "Oooh, it was awful."

"How many people?" asked the old man, hanging up the phone.

"I don't know," said the other. "I only looked at one of the cars. That's all I had to do."

"It's awful," said the old man. "Just awful. Makes you kind of sick."

"Yes, it does," said the younger man and suddenly he ran outside and went behind the building and vomited.

After a few minutes he went into the station washroom and rinsed out his mouth, and then felt the need for a pickup and went back inside and had a bottle of root beer.

In a few minutes a highway patrol car whined past the station at great speed.

"There they go," said the old man.

"What happened?" asked the child.

"Nothing, honey," the old man said. "You go on and play. Your ma'll be back soon."

Another car stopped outside and a man and woman got out and walked briskly into the station.

"Has somebody called an ambulance?" the new man asked.

"Yes," said the proprietor. "It's all taken care of. The highway patrol just went out."

"We just saw them," said the woman, "but they'll need an ambulance, too."

"Must be one on the way," the old man said. "They got a radio in the police car."

"Oh, dear," said the woman. "What a sight."

"Yes," said the man from Michigan, "it was awful. I saw it a few minutes ago. Awful." He screwed up his face at the memory.

"Don't know what people mean, driving fast," said the old man.

"It's just awful," the man from Michigan repeated.

"You want to go back there, honey?" the new man said to the woman who stood behind him.

"No," she said, shuddering. "No, sir!"

"All right," he said. "Let's move on."

"Good-by," the old man said. "Thanks for stopping in."

"All right," said the new man as he left, closing the door.

"Just last month," the old man said. "One of them big trucks. Burned right up. Now this. I don't know what's going on these days."

"Yes, it's awful," said the man from Michigan. "Makes you sick."

Back at the scene of the wreck a dozen cars had stopped and pulled off the road. The highway patrolmen had put out flares and lanterns and a small red flag. Some of the passing drivers were out in the road in their shirt sleeves, ready to wave off on-coming traffic, willing to help if they could. Women sat in several of the cars, fearful.

"Looks like a head-on," one of the patrolmen said to the other.

"Yep. I've called for the ambulance. May take a few minutes."

The taller of the two took out a pad and pencil and began making notes.

"The Buick has New York plates," he said. "What's on the other car?"

"Utah plates," his companion said.

"A mess for the families, handling it long distance."

"Yeah."

"They all dead?"

"Pretty sure. This guy is, that's for certain. And the woman looks done for. Might be a chance for the driver of the Dodge, but I doubt it."

"Son-of-a-bitch," said the tall patrolman, shaking his head from side to side. "What can you do?"

"Yep," said his companion, "All right, you people there, keep over to the side. Over! Over! We've got to keep traffic moving through here, goddammit!"

"What happened, officer?" said a small man with a loud sport shirt and dark glasses.

"What do you think?" the patrolman said scornfully. "Keep out of the way there."

The small man stepped nimbly away and took a three-dimensional color camera out of a small leather case that hung by a strap over his shoulder. He walked carefully around the Buick and took three or four pictures, then walked down the road to the overturned Dodge and took two more. In a short time he had gathered a small group around him and set himself up as an authority.

"Must have happened right over there," he said. "You can see the Buick was going south."

"Is that right?" said a woman, pushing her hair out of her eyes.

"Yes, that's the way I figure it," the man with the camera said.

9

HOUSTON
INCIDENT

"*It's a long road that has no turning.*"

The man was middle-aged, over fifty, Mac guessed, and he had come up from the rear walking slowly, just fast enough to bring himself abreast of the boy. His face had a heavy stubble of beard and his wrinkled coat did not match his pants. Slightly drunk, he had the easy but ignominious grace of the professional panhandler. Mac expected him to ask for money.

"What did you say?"

"I say it's a long road that has no turning," the man repeated.

"Yep, I guess it is."

They walked along in silence for a few moments, Mac's stomach aching and gnawing on itself in the grip of hunger. He kept his eye on the curb. Once in a great while you could find a coin in the gutter, and a coin meant a loaf of bread or a candy bar or a carton of milk and the stopping of the pain in the stomach.

"You on the road?" the man said.

"Yes."

"Headed West?"

"That's right."

"The coast?"

"Yep."

More silence as they walked along in the pale Southern autumn sunlight, through the streets of Houston.

"Where you from?"

"Chicago."

The pavement pressed up hard against the soles of Mac's feet. He was tired of walking and his back ached.

"Hungry?"

"What?" His head spun at the thought of food. He suddenly developed the craft, the tight controlled excitement of the animal.

"I'm goin' in here for a cuppa coffee." The man indicated an open-air bar. "Want to join me?"

"Why, yes, I guess that wouldn't be a bad idea at that." He struggled to act casual.

They strolled in off the hot pavement, into the dim, musty half-saloon half-chili joint. Mac stared eagerly at the giant coffee-maker that gleamed and hissed against the wall, tasted with his eyes the rows of steaming frankfurters that lay in open trays behind the bar.

"Just a coffee," said his host.

"I'll have a coffee, too and . . . uh . . . I believe, a hot dog."

Wolfing it down, he closed his eyes and leaned back against the bar, feeling the wooden railing firm against his back. The coffee sloshed down his esophagus and curled out warmly along the lining of his stomach. The frankfurter meat was of poor quality, but he had never enjoyed turkey or a filet mignon more. He forced himself to take smaller bites as he neared the end of the sandwich.

"Care for another?"

"Why, yes, I think I might."

Twenty minutes later he was finishing his fifth hot dog and his third cup of coffee.

"You look like you could use a bath, Slim."

In a fatherly way the man slipped his arm around Mac's shoulder and looked into his face.

"Yes, sir. I figured soon as I saw you, I said, here's a boy, I said, who could use a good bath. Not that he's the kind who wouldn't take one if he could, I said, but here's the kind of a boy who just hasn't had a chance lately."

The man's whiskyish breath caused Mac to draw back a bit and as he did so a gnarled, brown-spotted hand patted him affectionately on the thigh. Mac took his foot off the bar rail and inched away. There was something weird about this operator, but a bath . . . a bath would be the most welcome thing in the world now that he had filled his stomach. A bath and a good shave would put him back on top of the world. Even if he had to put his filthy clothes back on, at least his body would be clean underneath them.

"My hotel's just around the corner," the man said as they left the bar. He put his arm up over Mac's worn suède jacket-back. A wave of revulsion swept him and he started to say, "Ixnay," but then he realized he might hurt the man's feelings. Without seeming to notice the man's arm he quickened his step so that he slipped away and the offending arm dropped of its own weight.

Going up in the elevator, he noticed that the attendant's uniform was greasy and torn. The building smelled ancient, dirty. The room was on the eighth floor and as soon as the man unlocked the door he walked in and poured himself a drink from a half-empty bottle on the dresser.

"Care for a snifter?" he said.

"No, thanks."

"You don't like me." Mac felt a quick chill, as of fear, go through him. He was in no mood for an emotional scene, least of all for one the full significance of which he did not, because of his tender years, understand.

"You don't like me, do you?" the man repeated, with a twisted smile.

"Why, certainly," Mac said, hedging. "What makes you think I've got anything against you? I'm very grateful to you, as a matter of fact, for the hot dogs and the coffee and everything."

"All right," the man said. "I just thought maybe you

didn't like me." He slumped on the bed and waved a welcoming hand around the room. "Go ahead," he said. "Make yourself at home. Take your bath."

"Where's the john?" Mac said.

"At the end of the hall."

"How do I get down there?"

"Oh, it's all right. You can just put a towel around yourself. There's never anybody in the hall in the afternoon."

Self-consciously Mac sat on a chair across the room and took off his shoes and socks. Then, standing, he removed his jacket, sweater, shirt, and pants.

"I'll wear my underwear down the hall," he said. "Do you have a towel and soap?"

"Sure," the man said, "but first why don't you have a little drink?"

"No, thanks, really. If it's all the same to you, I'd just as soon take the bath first." He didn't know why he had said *first*. It implied that he would be willing to have a drink later and he had no taste for liquor. He wanted to take a bath and then leave the hotel. He wanted to get away from the man, but strangely he could feel no anger in his heart, no actual ill will against the half-drunk unfortunate who leered at him blankly from across the room. He felt, rather, pity. He wanted to avoid offending the man. He wanted to avoid an argument.

In the shower he forgot the stranger and laughed aloud in the sheer exultation of the moment. The hot water streamed through his hair, hit his face, splashed down over his body as he lathered and turned and luxuriated in its blood-cheering warmth.

He thought of a line from Rupert Brooke . . . *the benison of hot water*. He laughed again, mouth turned up to catch the hot spray, eyes blinking, staring up into the needle holes in the spout, lathering his itching stomach, his loins, sudsing his hair, rinsing it, sudsing it again and again, feeling clean and strong, blinking, gasping, singing, standing like a savage in a monsoon, letting the water clean him out down to his soul, watching triumphantly as dirty suds washed down his legs, filtered off into the outlet on the floor. He sudsed his hair again, lathering his whole body, lifting his arms and his face to the warm, delicious torrent, poking his slippery fingers into his ears and washing his face again and again till his eyes stung from the soap.

He stood with bowed head under the water for at least another ten minutes, reluctant to give up the sensation. He was standing thus, almost asleep, when the shower curtain was jerked violently to one side.

"Howdy, big fella," the man said, stepping partly into the shower. He put his hand out and touched Mac's hip. Water dotted his sleeve.

"Hey, wait a minute! That's enough. I mean, this is no place to get smart."

"What's the matter?" The man seemed drunker, more desperate.

"Why, nothing's the matter. I just want to finish up taking this shower, that's all. Now just relax and go on

138

back to your room. I'll be back there in a couple of minutes."

Pouting slightly, the man retreated.

"I didn't mean no harm," he said.

His heart pounding, Mac turned off the water and dried himself. In his underwear he slipped back down the hall. It would be difficult now. The stranger had made his move.

"Feel better?"

"Yes, thanks," reaching for the trousers, slipping into them. "That bath really hit the spot."

"What's your hurry? Wouldn't you like to catch a little shut-eye?"

"Well, to tell you the truth, I really would, but I'll tell you . . . I . . . I have to go mail a letter."

The excuse was so lamely offered they avoided looking at each other for a moment. Then the man started to sob.

"You don't like me," he said, sniffling. "I told you before you didn't. I knew it."

"Aw, don't cry. I like you all right. It's just that I have to get out of here and mail these letters."

"But you won't come back." He had the pathetic expression of an about-to-be-abandoned dog.

"Sure I will." Anything to get away.

"No, you won't. I bought you all those hot dogs and the coffee and fixed you up here so you could take a shower and everything and now you're sore and you won't come back." The man rubbed the back of his hand across his nose and belched. Then he rose and poured himself another drink, whimpering.

"Don't cry," Mac said. "See, here are the letters I'm talking about." He pulled two letters out of the pocket of his jacket. "I'm not kidding. I really have to mail them." He sat down on the chair and put on his stockings and shoes as quickly as he could, his fingers trembling.

"I don't know, what the hell," the man said, sobbing and looking at the floor.

His hand on the doorknob Mac turned and tried to smile reassuringly. A heartfelt sorrow for the man was mingled with his disgust.

"Thanks," he said. "Thanks for everything. You take it easy here and I'll go mail these letters and if I get a chance I'll drop back a little later. I really will if it's possible."

Without waiting for an answer, he closed the door and walked swiftly down the hall to the elevator, listening to see if the man would follow. In a moment he was out in the street. The sun was lower in the sky. He turned toward it, walking very briskly, and stepped out into the street, walking parallel to the curb, lifting his thumb to passing cars.

10

THE LATE
MR. ADAMS

*M*r. *Adams, to get right to the point, was born* late. The doctor had solemnly wiped his spectacles, pursed his lips, made the sort of face all doctors are supposed to make after wiping their spectacles and pursing their lips, and announced that George Adams would be born on August 23.

On August 22 his mother felt pains and retired to await George's arrival. On August 29 the doctor suggested light housework and a change of diet, re-examined his calculations, and stated with assured finality that George would be born within two days. George was born seven days later.

Till the day he died George loved to tell the story of his long-delayed arrival, and I suppose psychologists might suggest that his lifelong addiction to tardiness was a subconscious means of recapturing the glory, such as it was, that was his on the occasion of his birth.

They say that the worst thief in the world is an honest man ninety-nine per cent of the time. They say that except on certain days of the week Hitler wasn't an altogether unlikable sort of chap. They say that all beautiful women have their unattractive moments, that saints sometimes sin, and that the New York Yankees don't always defeat their opponents from Philadelphia.

They say that nobody runs entirely true to type. But they are wrong. George Adams was late coming into this world, he was late being weaned, he was late learning to speak, he was late for school habitually from the first day he attended kindergarten, and with very rare exceptions he was late for every blessed appointment of any importance that was ever included in his busy schedule.

His other vices, fortunately, were few and of relative unimportance, and his virtues were many. He always managed somehow to discharge his educational responsibilities with ease, and when he graduated from the state university he was in the upper tenth of his class.

He was, needless to say, tardy in arriving at the graduation ceremony, but his dean was in no way surprised by this circumstance, and George's diploma was handed to him privately after the speech-making and singing had ended and the janitors were beginning to fold up the auditorium chairs and put them away.

George's father soon thereafter made an opening at his plant and George filled it neatly. His father, with great wisdom, instructed George's secretary to deliberately lie to George regarding the times of all especially important business appointments, so that when George had to meet a business associate for lunch at one o'clock he usually was given the impression that the engagement was set for twelve-thirty, and so when he sauntered onto the scene at something like twelve fifty-four there was really no harm done.

George made a great many friends as a junior executive and in no time was promoted and given a substantial increase in income. While not handsome he was more than slightly attractive, women found him amusing, and so one day when he announced that he was engaged to be married the news was not entirely unexpected.

His father, fortunately, had the presence of mind to warn George's bride that her husband-to-be might arrive a few minutes late for the wedding service, so although she was visibly annoyed by this eventuality when it came to pass, she was not driven to tears and there was really no scene at all. Besides, George had the best of excuses: he had stopped to have his car washed and to make a long-distance telephone call to a hotel in New York to make absolutely certain the honeymoon suite had been reserved.

George usually had a good excuse, as a matter of fact. He wasn't late on purpose; his intentions were the best in the world. It was just that most of the time, what with one thing and another coming up at the last minute, he never quite seemed to get anywhere as early as he wanted to.

In later years George came to be a prominent citizen

of the town, and there was even talk one year of running him for mayor. He declined this honor, however, and continued to devote himself to private endeavor. After his father died he assumed the presidency of the plant and rendered the company distinguished service. His marriage withal was a happy one and his children, four in number, were a fine-looking group at the funeral not long ago.

Everyone said it was one of the nicest funerals in recent years, and though George's family was heart-broken, you could see they were still able to feel a glow of pride as they looked over the crowd that packed into the church to pay its respects and hear the funeral oration.

I suppose there must have been many in the crowd who were aware that, in dying, George Adams was early for almost the first time in his life. His physician, who had detected a serious heart condition, had given him two years to live, at the outside; and the good doctor was as shocked as the townspeople when, three weeks after his examination, diagnosis, and prediction, his patient quietly passed away in his sleep.

The caravan of sleek, black limousines winding to the cemetery was imposing, indeed, and the casual passers-by must have concluded that a very important personage was being laid to rest.

One minor mishap interrupted the smooth flow of events, incidentally, at what was, to all practical purposes, the very last minute. The hearse that carried George's coffin must have run over a nail in the road, for one of its tires went suddenly quite flat and the driver and his assistant pulled over to the roadside to replace it with a spare. After a hasty conference it was decided that all the other cars should proceed, as planned, directly to the burial ground. This they did and the mourners, stepping out of the limousines sedately, clustered around the Adams plot and stood conversing in whispers, waiting for George.

He arrived only twenty-three minutes late.

11

THE JUDGMENT

Solomon had been in Jerusalem for seven days. During that time he had daily burned lambs and offered them to the Lord.

Twenty-four hours after he had returned from Gibeon he had declared a feast for his servants and friends; the gesture had done much to promote his popularity. The dream at Gibeon had convinced Solomon that the people would welcome an ostentatious manifestation of his leadership. He was determined to be a wise and good king, young as he was, and to do all in his power to emulate the example of his father, David.

On the first day after the feast Ahilud brought before him two women.

"What is this?" Solomon demanded, when Ahilud

walked into the courtyard. "I did not send for these two."

"Forgive me, my lord," said Ahilud, "but these cackling fowl have caused much dissension in the neighborhood and I would appreciate a decision from your lordship as to how we might put an end to their bickering."

"Can I not enjoy a quiet cup of wine on a warm afternoon without being interrupted with trifles?"

"My apologies, my lord," Ahilud said, motioning to the two to withdraw.

For the first time Solomon looked at them. One was quite pretty, young, black-haired, and sullen. The other appeared to be slightly older. Her figure was fuller and beneath her robes she shifted her weight from one leg to the other awkwardly under Solomon's gaze.

"Wait," said the king. "Who are these women?"

"They are harlots, my lord," answered Ahilud with a slight smile.

"Indeed," said Solomon. "What sport is this you are making, Ahilud, that the king should be obliged to settle an argument between whores?"

"Meaning no disrespect," said Ahilud with an almost imperceptible bow, "but the subject of their argument has caught the fancy of the people. There has been some little demand that your wisdom be employed in the settlement of this—er—unusual difficulty."

"As much as it pains me to admit it," Solomon said drily, "I am afraid my curiosity has been piqued."

"Speak," said Ahilud, prodding the ribs of the woman closest to him.

"My lord," said the woman, the older of the two, "this woman and I dwell in one house."

"Just the two of you?"

"Yes."

"Go on."

"I was delivered of a child with her in the house."

"Yes."

"And it came to pass that the third day after I was delivered, this woman was delivered also."

Solomon lifted one eyebrow slightly and looked at Ahilud.

"Well," he said, stroking his chin to hide a smile. "You were alone, you say?"

"There was no stranger with us in the house. No one save we two."

"I see."

Casting a hateful glance at the younger woman, the fuller-hipped one continued.

"Not long ago this woman's child died in the night."

Solomon clucked his tongue against his teeth sympathetically.

"She overlaid it with cloths and it smothered, I suppose," the woman said.

"Liar!" hissed the younger girl.

"Silence," said Ahilud, stepping forward.

"She arose at midnight," the woman continued triumphantly, "and took my son from me, while thy handmaid slept, my lord, and laid it at her bosom."

"And her child?"

"Her dead child she laid at *my* bosom."

"Liar," said the second woman in a loud voice. "Do not believe her, my lord. This is an evil tale she has invented to cheat me of my own flesh and blood."

"Please," said Solomon, wearily raising a hand, "please."

"When I rose in the morning to give my child suck," continued the woman, "behold it was dead, but when I looked at it closely in the light of day, behold, it was not my son, not the child I bore."

"No, my lord," said the younger. "Please believe me. The living child is my son."

"Witch," the woman cried. "Jealous, deceiving witch! The dead child is thy son! The living child is my son!"

"Enough," roared Solomon. "I am tired of the sound of your voices. There is one simple way to put an end to this silly argument."

"What is that, my lord?" said Ahilud.

"It is simplicity itself," said Solomon. "If the second child were to die, these haggling harlots would have nothing to argue about. They could return to their business and perhaps in time give birth again."

"Your suggestion?"

"Bring me a sword."

"A sword?"

"There is nothing wrong with your ears, Ahilud."

"Yes, my lord."

Walking to the doors of the courtyard, Ahilud removed a broad-bladed battle sword from its resting place on the inner wall. In a moment he returned to Solomon's chair.

"Witch!" the older woman exploded. "See what you have done now! The child is to be killed."

"That is correct," said Solomon. "Ahilud, with this sword divide the child in two. Give half to one of these women and half to the other."

At that the younger of the women threw herself on her knees at Solomon's feet.

"Oh, my lord," she cried, "please, I beg of you, give her the living child. Do not slay it."

"Hypocrite," snapped the other, wild-eyed, her face a mask of spite. "Pretender! By the Almighty, rather than see you fool the king with your deceitful tears I say let the child be neither mine nor thine."

"What?" gasped the dark-haired girl.

"Divide it," the woman answered hysterically, looking at Ahilud. "You will find the child in our house at this moment."

"Hold," said Solomon. "It is now an easy matter to see which of you is the true mother of the child."

Pointing to the younger woman, he said to Ahilud, "Give *her* the living infant. She could not allow it to be put to death. She is the child's mother."

"It shall be done, my lord," said Ahilud.

"But, my lord . . ." the older woman broke in.

"Enough," cried Ahilud. "The king is finished with you! Not another word or you shall be punished."

Before the sun had gone down on the day many people had heard of the king's wisdom and the cleverness of his method. The story was eventually told in all the corners of Israel, to Solomon's great honor, and is recounted to this day. Unfortunately no one can recall the name of the subtle and guileful young prostitute who outwitted a king and was permitted to bring up the child of another woman.

12

THE GADARENE
SWINE

The back of the donkey between Daniel's legs felt hot and hard. The morning sun was warm on his shoulders. Daniel half closed his eyes, dozing as he rocked along, the slight breeze from the lake moving freshly through the sweat-moistened wisps of his beard.

There had been a storm in the night and the rain had fallen even during the early hours of morning, but now the sky was clear and only a few scattered pools gave evidence that there had been a downpour.

To the left of the road the swine stood scattered in small knots against the side of the hill, the swineherds moving among them, threatening, shouting, moving them slowly and indirectly along the green face of the rise, toward the city and the market of the Gentiles.

The shrill cries of the robed figures that directed the

course of the herd mingled in Daniel's ears with the innocent, bubbly mutterings of the pigs. All in all the sound was a happy one, for such a fine, large herd would bring good prices in the city. For a few minutes Daniel wondered if perhaps he had erred in not accepting the offer of the Romans to buy up the entire lot for delivery to the garrison to the west of the city. But no, although it would take at least five days to sell the herd in small lots in the public market, in the end the profit would be almost twice as great and with the extra money he could afford to sink the new well for which the family had insistently clamored during the past year.

Shading his eyes, he looked off to the right of the road, down toward the water's edge, and frowned. Far ahead, perhaps half a mile, a crowd was gathered.

"Hallo," he cried, waving his arms to attract the attention of the swineherds. At the sudden trumpet blast of his voice against the morning stillness the donkey shied and flattened its ears.

"Look," called Daniel, his voice carrying up the side of the hill on the wind. Reining in his mount, he pointed to the throng in the distance.

"Take them up higher," he shouted. Some of the pigs were traveling ahead in the roadway, and if the herd were not brought up and around so as to avoid coming into contact with the hangers-on in the back of the mob, there might well be a number of porkers stolen in the confusion.

With much flapping and shouting the herdsmen began

154

slipping down the hill below the pigs, forcing them to higher ground. It would be all right, Daniel decided after a few minutes' consideration. The pigs were now traveling well to the left of the road, except for a handful of stragglers and now he had to shout again to admonish the herdsmen not to hurry them too much. A stampede or even a noticeable acceleration in the pace of the herd would melt valuable weight off the fat backs and heavy hocks which careful feeding had built up at such great cost during the long winter months and upon which Daniel was depending for the profits that would enable him to exist and expand in the coming year.

Approaching the crowd, Daniel drew his sleeve across his brow and dug his heels gently into the ribs of the donkey.

He could not as yet determine the nature or purpose of the assemblage milling along the bench ahead of him. Perhaps they had gathered to witness a scene of violence, a fight between two men, or the body of a traveler waylaid by bandits. Or perhaps something interesting had been washed up out of the sea.

He would not have long to tarry with the crowd, Daniel knew but, overcome by curiosity, he urged the ass forward at a brisk walk and at last was able to perceive that the attention of the throng was directed upon one man who stood a little distance apart on a small rise, preaching in a loud voice.

Coming at last to the part of the road that was blocked by those in the back of the crowd, Daniel dismounted and addressed a tall, gaunt man standing attentively with his head turned slightly to one side, a hand cupped to his ear.

"Who is the preacher?" Daniel said.

"I do not know," the man answered, "from here it is difficult to hear him."

At this moment a shout went up from a number of people in the center of the crowd and was carried to the outer edges of the gathering like ripples produced by a rock thrown into a pool.

"What has happened?" someone shouted.

"It is the man from out of the tombs," a voice explained. "He is being taken before the Master."

"Who is the man from out of the tombs?" Daniel said to the tall stranger.

"I know not," the man answered. "Perhaps he is one possessed or crippled or dying. From this far back one cannot hear."

"I am going to attempt to get in closer around the side," Daniel said and, leading the donkey, he walked around to the right of the crowd. A stunted olive tree stood before him and with a sudden inspiration he brought the ass up close under the tree and, bracing himself by holding one of the scrawny branches, he stood up full length upon the animal's back.

Now, he was happy to learn, it was possible for him to see and hear reasonably well all that took place.

In the center of the crowd a group of four men were constraining a fifth, a ragged derelict, who towered over them and lifted up his voice, demanding to be set free.

"Let us through," shouted one of the four. "We must bring this man before the Master."

The crowd fell back like chaff blown before the wind, but the prisoner braced himself and pulled his captors off balance.

"Unhand me," he cried. "You are trying to kill me. I have done nothing. Release me!"

Suddenly the man who had been preaching walked briskly into the mob and approached the knot of struggling men.

"Peace," he cried commandingly. "What has happened?"

"Master," explained a man at his heels, "this man is one possessed. He lives among the tombs and has endangered all who have dared to approach. He is very strong and capable of much evil."

"So?" said the preacher.

"What have I to do with thee, Jesus?" cried the wild-eyed prisoner. Then, mockingly, he shouted, "Thou Son of the most high God, I adjure thee by God that thou torment me not!"

The preacher made no immediate answer but regarded the man levelly for perhaps half a minute. Gradually the captive ceased his struggles and gazed back quizzically but without changing the contemptuous twist of his mouth.

Then the preacher pointed at him and said in a loud, clear voice, "Come out of the man, thou unclean spirit!"

At this the imprisoned one threw back his head and uttered a piercing scream that was part laughter.

"What is thy name?" said the preacher.

"My name," the man spat back, rolling his eyes wildly, "is Legion, for we are many."

Some in the crowd now fell on their knees in wonder.

The four who held the arms of the sick man were now tossed about again by his struggles, but they held fast and did not allow him to break free. Like a trapped wolf he looked over his shoulder and now directed the attention of the preacher to the herd of swine that had stopped to graze close by upon the hillside. Throwing back his head again, he moaned loudly and shouted, "Send us into the swine that we may enter into them!"

Looking up into the heavens, the preacher made a sweeping gesture with his right hand and pointed to the herd. The crowd broke and ran to the right and the left and Daniel, gripped by a sudden mighty fear, slipped down upon the donkey and urged it into a trot. It was not clear to him what was about to happen, but he was seized with panic that harm might befall the herd, and he began to wave his arms in signal to the herdsmen standing far up the side of the hill.

By now a great roar had gone up from the mob and with horror Daniel perceived that the pigs closest to the road had begun to mill restlessly about.

"Make way," cried a voice from the mob and at that an ever-widening funnel-like opening was made in the center of the throng into which the pigs began streaming in a frenzied, grunting mass.

In vain Daniel tried to break through, to get in front of the stampeding herd, but within a matter of seconds the hillside was enveloped in a cloud of dust as hundreds of pigs shouldered their way downward toward the sea, screaming, shrieking, sounding like frightened humans.

Some splashed thunderously into the surf from the beach; others fell into the water by leaping from a slight rise that ended precipitously at the water's edge.

The preacher stood silently watching the suicidal rush of the panicked animals until the surface of the water was a seething, bubbling mass of flesh that squirmed and gasped and screamed in a peculiar womanlike manner, and then he turned his back upon the scene and stepped up upon the road that led to the city.

The crowd was beginning to disperse and it was not long before the story of what had happened was being told in the city. Many wondered and marveled and the fame of the preacher was greatly widespread thereby.

Daniel sat disconsolately by the side of the road for the rest of the afternoon, refusing to go either to the city or back to his home. There were tears in his eyes as he looked at the bodies of his pigs washed up on the shore, drying in the afternoon sun.

Simon, his chief herdsman, sat down beside him.

"Shall we try to bring buyers out from the city to sell what little we can?" he asked.

"No," said Daniel. "It would be of no avail. Pigs must be butchered and dressed quickly or in this heat the meat is no good. It is all a loss, a terrible loss."

"You are right," said Simon. "I fancy that already I can detect the smell of death floating up from the water's edge. We had best go away from this place and leave the job of cleaning up this mess to dogs and vandals and the wind and the sun and the rain. The area will be uninhabitable for months."

"You may go," said Daniel.

"And what of you?" asked Simon. "Will you be going home to tell your family about what has happened?"

"I must, I suppose, but I do not feel equal to the task right now. It is not an easy thing for a man to tell his wife and children that they have lost everything and will not soon have even enough to eat and drink."

Simon stared at the distant line separating water and sky.

"Everything," he said, "is assumed to have its purpose in the eternal scheme. I wonder what was the purpose of this strange occurrence."

"Who can say?" said Daniel. "The mind is at all times full of imponderables and mysterious questions. Who can say where the stars go when they go out? Who can say why evil exists? Who can even say," he muttered, almost to himself, "if the end justifies the means?"

13

THE SUNDAY
MORNING SHIFT

I didn't like being assigned to the Sunday-
morning shift. But I was the new man, so I had to take
it. Like anything else, it wasn't so bad once you got used
to it. It did mean you couldn't do much on Saturday
nights, but sometimes, driving in from the ocean on a
nice, cool Sunday morning with the streets deserted, and
the fog lifting off the lawns and palm trees, it was sort
of nice. You had the feeling you had the world all to
yourself.

I remember on Sunday mornings Los Angeles used to
look like it had in the old days, in the thirties, when
there were a lot of empty lots and pepper trees growing
wild and orange-juice stands and for-rent signs. The
boom of the war years did something bad to Los Angeles as far as just simple living was concerned. The

town had gotten overcrowded, more industrial, smoggier, pushier, noisier: more Eastern.

But on Sunday mornings it was, as I say, a lot like the old Los Angeles. Quiet. Peaceful. You felt like taking deep breaths as you drove along.

Of course, working the Sunday-morning shift, you couldn't go to church. But it was all right, in a way, because church came to you. You opened up the station at about ten minutes to six, said good morning to the janitor and the engineer, went to the record library, picked up the records you needed, if any, went to the announcer's booth, and that was about it. At six o'clock you signed the station on the air and it was pretty much of a snap from then till twelve, when the Sunday-afternoon man came on.

Weekdays you had to be on your toes every minute, what with playing records, doing newscasts, reading a million and one commercials and all, but on Sundays there were very few records to play, there was only one brief newscast at nine o'clock, and you didn't have to do any commercials at all. Not that there weren't commercials to broadcast. The time was all sold solid, from six to noon, to various churches around the town, but the gentlemen of the cloth did their own commercials.

Some of the other radio announcers used to kid me about working for KTLB. We were known as the Bible Station, which is certainly better than poking yourself in the eye with a sharp stick, but the other announcers meant it as a plain insult. You see, the rest of the week we did pretty much the same job as the other independ-

ents in town: records and news. But during a slump just
before the war old Charlie Young, who used to own
KTLB, found the used-car dealers and supermarkets
weren't buying much time, so out of desperation or
something he cut prices a little and made some sales to
a few of the clergy. The first boys to get on really had
a field day, and then the rest of them began to buy time
and before Charlie knew it he found himself with a
pretty big church business.

When I say church, of course, I don't mean Episco-
palian or Catholic or Methodist or anything like that.
The outfits we had broadcasting on Sundays were pretty
much Los Angeles-type churches, if you know what I
mean, and if you've never lived in Los Angeles I guess
you don't. For some reason LA has become the nut
center of the world. I don't mean pecans and walnuts,
I mean flippo-time. Nuts in the head style. Don't ask me
why. That's one for the brainy people to figure out, but
man, there are more weirdos walking the streets without
keepers in LA than in any city I've ever lived in and
I've lived in plenty, being a hack announcer. I've worked
in Pittsburgh, Des Moines, Peoria, San Francisco, Santa
Barbara, and Seattle. LA beats 'em all. People there
don't seem to be like people in other places. Oh, that's
an exaggeration, I guess. Maybe the majority of people
are pretty much the same all over, but I guess it's just
that the percentage of odd-balls is higher on the Coast
than elsewhere. You see an awful lot of health-food
stores, revival tents, lecture halls where nobody in his
right mind can figure out what the hell the lecturers are

lecturing about, hospitals that medical societies keep trying to get closed up, and churches with names like Church of the Holy Triangle (Spirit, Love, and Health) and Church of the Atomic Christ and Church of the Living Holy Ghost and things like that.

I think maybe one reason things are so peculiar along this line is that Los Angeles is a city where lots of people go to live after they've really finished living and don't know it and aren't quite ready to lay down and die. So they go out there and with all this free time on their hands and maybe being in their old age where their health isn't too good, they fall easy prey to the vultures that infest the city.

Anyway, a lot of these evangelists had bought time on KTLB and on Sunday mornings it was my job to put them on the air. An engineer would give 'em one of the studios, and from the announcer's booth I'd play an opening theme record (always some organ music) and read their introductions out of the copy book. It was always something like: "The Wilshire Boulevard Church of the New Prophecy is on the air! Yes, friends, once again it's time for one of your Sunday-morning visits to the Shrine of New Prophecy [with the organ music still going] and another inspiring sermon by Dr. Homer Crockett. With Dr. Crockett this morning you'll hear the choir in a medley of your favorite hymns of yesteryear. And now, Dr. Crockett."

Most of the ministers who had taken to the airways were pretty nice guys personally and, for all I know, they were as sincere as the day is long. But I said most.

Couple of those boys were confidence men for the Lord for sure, and oddly enough they were more interesting, if you know what I mean, than the honest ones. I mean they were better speakers; they had better vocabularies. They could get themselves more wound up in a sermon. And they could pull in more money.

That's the purpose, of course, of broadcasting church services. It's not the only purpose, but it's one of the main ones and in a way it's perfectly easy to understand. You see, even on a small station radio time costs a lot of money. Most of these fellows ordinarily couldn't have afforded it if they tried to pay for time-costs out of what they took in with the collection baskets at their churches. Their real source of income was from all the folks out in what we used to call radioland. That's the reason why a few minutes of each broadcast period would be allotted to a frank appeal for funds. Some of the fellas used to ask for the money sort of bashfully, as if they were ashamed to have to bring the subject up. But not old Mort Fairview. How about that for a name? Dr. Morton *Fairview*. I don't know where he got it, but I bet he wasn't born with it. It was a good name for his purposes though. You had to hand it to him. He didn't overlook a trick.

He's the fellow I started to tell you about. In a way he made the Sunday-morning shift interesting. At least he saved it from being a total loss. He had several gimmicks that—well, let me tell you how he operated.

First of all, he bought the eleven o'clock time. More people awake than at six or seven. Then he didn't talk just simple Sunday-school stuff like most of the other clergymen who broadcast on the station. He'd get up plenty of steam. He'd take on Russia or the devil or sin or atheism or something and really tear it apart. He also used to buy newspaper space in the Saturday papers and advertise sermons entitled "Rome versus Moscow" and "666" and "The Vatican and the White House," but he used to go easy on the anti-Catholic stuff when he was on the air. He seemed to be the only one of the Sunday-morning bunch who realized that one way to get ahead in this world is to give people something to hate. You tell 'em there's something they ought to hate, and then you hate it right out loud to show them how, and then you tell the people to tear off a little piece for themselves, and then you all get to hating together and, man, you can really do all right if you know the ropes. That's the way Fairview used to work it.

I had to admire him. When he wasn't calling fire and brimstone down on some common enemy, he used to do the greatest sleight-of-hand with words you ever heard in your life. He practically used to convince me that what he was saying made a lot of sense till I would try to concentrate very hard on the meaning of his words and then I'd be aware that there was no meaning.

He was a natural-born salesman, was what he was. He would have made a great used-car man or a great Senator or a great football coach or a great anything. How he got with the religious dodge I don't know, but that's beside the point. He had the simple old gift of gab. After listening to him for about six months, though,

I finally got on to some of his tricks. One of them was what I called the "How many ways can you say it?" routine. That isn't a very good way to explain it, so I'll give you an example. He'd be going along doing sort of a normal sermon for a minute or two and then he'd happen to land on a phrase like *The Lord is a rock* and he'd be off.

He'd say, "The Lord is a rock in time of storm. He's a rock in time of strife. He's a rock in time of darkness. He's a rock in the middle of the sea. He's a rock in the desert. The Lord is a rock to cling to, a rock to hide behind, a rock to rest upon, a rock to build upon, a rock to stand upon, a rock to count on, a rock to plant on, a rock to tower up, a rock to shine forth, a rock to give you strength, a rock to give you safety, a rock to give you protection, a rock to give you love, a rock to lift you up, a rock to bring you peace." Man, he'd come on like a quarry for about five minutes with the rock routine.

Then he'd switch to something else: "The blood of the Lamb was shed for you. The blood of the Lamb was shed for me. The blood of the Lamb will wash you. The blood of the Lamb will cleanse you. The blood of the Lamb will feed you. The blood of the Lamb will revive you. The blood of the Lamb will thrill you. The blood of the Lamb will give you strength. The blood of the Lamb will nourish you. The blood of the Lamb will quench your thirst. The blood of the Lamb will soothe your pain. The blood of the Lamb will open your eyes. The blood of the Lamb will wash away your sins. The blood of the Lamb will make you free. The blood of the Lamb will put love in your heart. The blood of the Lamb will give you new understanding."

As the saying goes, it's a free country, and I'd be the last man in the world to clap a hand over the Doc's mouth, but if that's teaching people religion then that's what makes horse races. The Doc's sermons always sounded to me like they were written by the guy who wrote "Sh'Boom." Funny thing was, though, they sort of got to you, you know what I mean? Fairview himself was such a commanding guy that you just couldn't help getting carried away a little if you listened to him for a few minutes.

He'd bring three or four people with him to do a little singing, and after he'd get himself up to full speed they'd start with the "Yeah" and "Amen" routine and quite a lot of emotion used to come pouring out of that little Studio B.

Another thing I've always felt about the Doc is that he really ad-libbed all those sermons. Most of the other men used to bring scripts or notes or Bibles or something, but Fairview would just start talking and take it from there. "I met a man the other day," he might say, "and he said to me, 'Doctor Fairview, I'm sick. I'm sick of heart and mind and body. I'm sick of soul and I'm sick of bone and blood and marrow.' " I used to think that whatever it was that people said when they walked up to Fairview on the street it sure wasn't anything like that; but as I say, it didn't matter what kind of malarky Doc handed out, you just sort of went along with him. His eyes were so open and so blue and his face so red and good-natured and his hair was so white that, while you were looking at him, you just couldn't find it in yourself to doubt him or criticize him. It was only later that you looked at yourself in the mirror, so to speak, and realized that you hadn't come away with one single idea that you could put your finger on.

This one particular Sunday morning that I'm telling you about, though, the Doc really topped himself. I was sitting there in my swivel chair, with my feet up on the board, watching him through the glass panel of Studio B, listening to him and sort of dozing a little when suddenly he said he was going off the air.

"My friends," he said, "I have a shocking bit of news for you today. This program, which has brought the word of God to the people of this community for so many years . . . this program, which has brought so much comfort to so many troubled hearts, is going off the air. I had hoped I would never come to this moment, after all the wonderful support you grand folks out there in radioland have given me these past years, but this is the moment. This is my Gethsemane. This is my cross, and I must bear it. I have had a talk with the people who run this station. They are good people. They are fair people. They are upstanding American people. But they are not idle millionaires. They are not fools. They are ordinary people like you and me. People with families. People with bills to pay. Yes, a radio station has bills just as you and I do. They have to pay for the electricity they use. They have to pay salaries. They have to pay for typewriters and papers for scripts and janitors' salaries, and they have to pay for recordings and news-machines and transmitters and broadcasting towers and millions of miles of wires and tubes and connections and plugs and sockets and parts of all sorts. This all takes money. That's why they can't afford to just *give* their broadcasting time away. I had a talk with them the other day and they told me they were very sorry, that they enjoyed my program and were very proud to be the station over which it was broadcast, but they said that as much as they sympathized with me, as much as they sympathized with my bringing the Word of God to the people of Los Angeles, they would, nevertheless, regretfully have to ask me to give up the time of this broadcast on next Sunday morning.

"For you see, my friends, these are troubled times we are living in. The cost of everything is going up. I don't have to tell you that. You know the cost of milk is up. The cost of bread is up. Rents are up. Everything is up. And my friends, the cost of broadcasting time is up, and I . . . I hesitate to say it . . . but it is a fact; I cannot afford it. That's right, my dear friends. I lay the facts before you. I cannot pay what it would cost me to buy one half-hour of time on this station next Sunday morning. I have spoken to the people who run this station and they were wonderful people, but after all they run a business. They cannot give away their commodity, time, any more than a butcher could give away meat or a lumberman give away wood, and still stay in business. So that's it, my friends. I am terribly sorry to have to say good-by to you after these many long years. I have gotten to know a great many of you personally these past few years. Some of you I have known by your letters, others by your personal visits to my Tabernacle. I have heard your stories, I have suffered with you in your time of strife, I have prayed for you in sickness and in all sorts of unhappiness. And now, in one terrible moment of time, all is lost. Nevermore are we . . . you and I . . . to know each other so intimately by the wonderful magic of radio that God in His goodness and mercy has deigned to give to a needy world to spread all manner of good and happy tidings. Ah, what a wonderful gift radio is, my friends. What a comfort it is to shut-ins, to the infirm, the aged, the lonely. What a godsend it is to all of us . . . to you and to me. For it has been by the miracle of radio, beloved friends, that I have been able to bring you the holy word for such a long time. But now, in one tragic moment, all this is swept away. In one sad announcement I am reciting the news of my doom. Or rather not my own doom but the doom of my work or my mission in life. But ours not to reason why. Perhaps God in His goodness and wisdom will show me the purpose behind the tragedy. Perhaps He will let me know for what cause I have struggled so long. I am sure He will. And yet perhaps I betray Him if I give up so easily. It is difficult to tell what to do, my friends. Perhaps I should turn to you. What do *you* think I should do? You, who have so often turned to me for advice, now *I* am turning to *you*. What poetic justice! And what a wonderful testimony to God's wisdom. How He shows us that we help ourselves best by helping others. Will you help me, my friends? Is it possible that is what God is doing this morning? Testing you as you sit there listening in Los Angeles and Glendale and Burbank and Santa Monica and Eagle Rock and in all the wonderful sections of this great city of ours? Is that His grand and glorious purpose? I do not know, my friends.

"*Is* He testing you? Will you help? Do you feel any call at all this morning? Do you feel that God is giving you a very special opportunity to help Him spread His holy word? Is there grace in your heart this morning? Is there love? Is there joy? Is there gratitude? Is there the love of God and all His creatures? Is there the love for the little creatures of this earth? The love for the little blue-eyed children who may be denied the word of God if they do not one morning hear it over this microphone? Is there love and compassion in your heart this morning? It is written . . . *faith, hope, and charity, and the greatest of these is charity*. You know your Bible. You know the word. Is there charity in your heart this morning? This grand and glorious California morning with the sun shining and the birds twittering in the trees. This morning when we all ought to get down on our knees and thank God for our many blessings. Why don't we do that? Why don't we do *just* that right now? Let's all get down on our knees right now, all over this great city, all over the ocean towns and in the mountains and in the valley. Are you on your knees in front of your radio right now? That's it. Kneel! Kneel before God! Feel His grace flowing into your heart right out of the radio. Isn't it a grand and glorious feeling? Isn't it grand? Aren't you grateful to the good God in His everlasting heaven? If you are, my friends, then perhaps there is yet hope. Perhaps there is a way whereby the word of God might yet be preserved in a heathen world. Perhaps the devil shall yet be banished from the temple and the money-changers cast out into the byways in terrible disgrace. Right now, my friends, if you are on your knees, and I can see that you *are* all over this wonderful city of ours, right now lift your right hand to heaven and promise, make a solemn vow, if you really feel the call, to save this program. Yes! You can do it and you alone. Don't wait for the other fellow. You can't expect God to perform miracles because you've been lazy. You've got to do your part. Right now make a vow to help and then, God love you, get up off your knees and go to your writing desks and put a love offering in an envelope. Address it to the Reverend Dr. Morton Fairview, Station KTLB, Los Angeles. That's all there is to it, my friends. It's up to you. Will you do that? Will you help the Lord? If you will, right now, out loud say, 'Yes, Lord.' "

The people in the room with Fairview all said, "Yes, Lord."

"Then," concluded the Doctor, "we'll see. I can't promise anything. It's in God's hands now. He knows. And in a few days I'll know. I'll know if I'll be back here with you for another wonderful visit next Sunday morning. If you tune in and don't hear me, be not of faint heart. It means you did your part, but you got no help from your fellow citizens. The seed fell upon barren ground. No growth sprang up. But if, in the infinite mercy of the Lord, there is a wonderful outpouring of generosity here these next few days, then, praise God, I shall be back with you, my friends. For now I count on your prayers. Help me. I pray you. Remember the mailing address: Dr. Morton Fairview, Station KTLB, Los Angeles."

The Doc and his followers got out of the studio before I could say good-by to him or offer him my sympathies and I had to go yank some news off the ticker and introduce the next program anyway, so I didn't give him much more thought for the moment.

At twelve o'clock Jack Norton replaced me.

"Don't forget your lunchbox," he said as I was leaving the control room.

"Thanks," I said. "Say, it's too bad about old Doc Fairview."

"What about him?" Jack said.

"He's through as of today," I said. "Couldn't meet the ante. Said he was checking off as of this morning unless his fans come up with some last-minute scratch."

"Say, that's right," Jack said. "I forgot you've only been with us for about six months."

"What do you mean?"

"Man, Fairview does this thing all the time. Every seven or eight months."

"Maybe he needs the money though."

"Are you kidding?" Jack said. "He's got this time bought and paid for for the next twelve months. He makes a good steady income, but every so often the people get lazy with the five-dollar bills. He does the going-off-the-air speech to wake 'em up."

It was still Sunday morning when I got back in the car. There was some traffic now, but not much. I drove back out to the beach at a good clip. I wanted to take the kids on a picnic.

14

THE PUBLIC
HATING

*T*he weather was a little cloudy and here and
there in the crowds that surged up the ramps into the
stadium, people were looking at the sky and then at their
neighbors and squinting and saying, "Hope she doesn't
rain."

On television the weatherman had forecast slight
cloudiness but no showers. It was not an unusual day for
early September. It was not cold. People from all over
town, about sixty-five thousand of them, were pouring
out of streetcars and buses and subways all over the
neighborhood surrounding the stadium. In antlike lines
they crawled across streets through turnstiles, up stair-
ways, along ramps, through gates, down aisles.

Laughing and shoving restlessly, damp-palmed with
excitement, they came shuffling into the great concrete

bowl, some stopping to go to the rest rooms, some buying pop-corn, some taking free pamphlets from the uniformed attendants.

Everything was free this particular day. No tickets had been sold for the event. The public proclamations had simply been made in the newspapers and on TV, and over sixty-five thousand people had responded.

For weeks, of course, the papers had been suggesting that the event would take place. All during the trial, even as early as the selection of the jury, the columnists had slyly hinted at the inevitability of the outcome. But it had only been official since yesterday. The television networks had actually got a slight jump on the papers. At six o'clock the government had taken over all network facilities for a brief five-minute period during which the announcement was made.

"We have all followed with great interest," the premier had said, looking calm and handsome in a gray double-breasted suit, "the course of the trial of Professor Ketteridge. Early this afternoon the jury returned a verdict of guilty. This verdict having been confirmed within the hour by the Supreme Court, in the interests of time-saving, the White House has decided to make the usual prompt official announcement. There will be a public hating tomorrow. The time: 2:30 P.M. The place: Yankee Stadium in New York City. Your assistance is earnestly requested. Those of you in the New York area will find——"

The voice had droned on, filling in other details, and

then the newspapers went to press with the complete details and, in the morning, the early editions included pictures captioned "Bronx couple first in line," and "Students wait all night to view hating" and "Early birds." The pictures showed several people standing in line outside the stadium or sitting on blankets on the sidewalk, reading papers and drinking coffee to pass the time.

By one-thirty in the afternoon there was not an empty seat in the stadium and people were beginning to fill up a few of the aisles. Special police began to block off the exits, and word was sent down to the street that no more people could be admitted. Hawkers slipped through the crowd selling cold beer and hot dogs. An engineer stepped shyly to an open microphone, tapped it with his fingernail, and said, "Hello, Mac. Testing. One, two. Woof, woof."

At this there was a smattering of applause followed by a ripple of laughter. An airplane droned overhead in the leaden sky and a slight breeze whipped the flags at the far end of the field.

Sitting just back of what would have been first base had the Yankees not been playing in Cleveland, Frederic Traub stared curiously at the platform in the middle of the field. It was about twice the size of a prizefighting ring. In the middle of it there was a small raised section on which was placed a plain wooden kitchen chair.

To the left of the chair there were seating accommodations for a small group of dignitaries. Downstage, so to speak, there was a speaker's lectern and a battery of microphones. The platform was hung with bunting and pennants.

"Remarkable," said Traub softly to his companion.

"I suppose," said the man. "Effective, at any rate."

Traub allowed his eye to wander from the platform to the bull pens, out over the brilliantly green playing field to the center-field bleachers. The crowd was beginning to hum ominously, like a lion audibly considering the possibility of going out to kill meat. Here and there cow bells rang out; sitting about twenty yards to the left Traub could see two Shriners standing up, addressing those in their immediate vicinity. He could not hear what they were saying.

At two minutes after two o'clock a small group of men filed out onto the field from a point just back of home plate. The crowd buzzed more loudly for a moment and then burst into applause. A military band struck up a brisk march, and two or three of the men in the group on the field could be observed to be making an effort to keep in step.

The applause had stopped before the group reached the platform. The men carefully climbed a few wooden steps, walked in single file across the platform, and seated themselves in the chairs set out for them. Traub turned around, rubbernecking, and was interested to observe, high in the press box, the winking red lights of television cameras.

"I didn't know you televised the thing," he said.

"Certainly," said his companion. "On all networks.

I think at one time only one network carried the event, but the program simply annihilated the competition, no joke intended, and they finally hit on the idea of having all the stations carry it. Only sensible way."

"I guess that's right," said Traub. "Still it all seems a little strange to me. We do things rather differently."

"That's what makes horse-racing," said his companion.

Traub listened for a moment to the voices around him. Surprisingly, no one seemed to be discussing the business at hand. Baseball, movies, the weather, gossip, personal small talk, a thousand-and-one subjects were introduced. It was almost as if the attempt to avoid a mention of the hating were deliberate.

"Think you'll be all right when we start?"

His friend's voice broke in on Traub's reverie.

"What?"

"Think you'll be okay when we get down to business?"

"Oh, certainly," said Traub. "Certainly."

"I've seen 'em keel over," said the other.

"I'll be all right," said Traub, shaking his head in admiring disbelief. "But I still can't believe it."

"What do you mean?"

"Oh, you know, the whole thing. How it started. How you found you could do it."

"Beats the hell out of me," said the other man. "I think it was that guy at Duke University first came up with the idea. The 'mind over matter' thing has been around for a long time, of course. Everybody from

Christ to Mary Baker Eddy has had a crack at it. But this guy, I forget what his name was, he was the first one to prove scientifically that mind can control matter."

"Did it with dice, I believe," Traub said.

"Yeah, that's it. First he found some guys who could drop a dozen or so dice down a chute of some kind and actually control the direction they'd take, at least control it to a small extent."

"I'm familiar with the experiments," said Traub, anxious to show that he was not in complete ignorance. "I believe the dice fell into a tray that was divided into two sections."

"Right," said his companion. "Anyway, some people could make a few more dice slide down into the right half of the tray, say, than chance would allow. After a few years they found out that the secret was real simple. The guys who had this particular power were nothing but the guys who *thought* they could do it."

"In other words," said Traub, half-smiling, "faith can move mountains."

"That's about the size of it," said the man. "Of course not many people could convince themselves they really had the knack of the damned thing, so nothing much was ever done with it. Then one time they got the idea of taking the dice into an auditorium and having about two thousand people concentrate on forcing the dice into one side of the tray or the other. That did it."

"Really?"

"You betcha. Why, hell, it was the most natural thing in the world when you think of it. It was so simple every body just overlooked it all those years. If one horse can pull a heavy load so far, it figures that ten horses can pull it a lot farther."

"Remarkable," said Traub.

"Anyway, that did it. They had them dice fallin' where they wanted 'em to go about eighty per cent of the time. Then some wise boy got the idea of trying a little mass hypnosis on the crowd before they tried the experiment, and it worked even better. Seems there'd been some in the crowd who didn't think they could do it, ya know. They were cuttin' the average way down. Well, when this boy got the people all excited, why, man, they really had themselves a crap game!"

"When did they first substitute a living organism for the dice?" Traub asked.

"Damned if I know," said the man. "It was quite a few years ago and at first the government sort of clamped down on the thing. It's still under strict Washington control, you understand."

"Of course."

"I was just a kid at the time but I do remember that the SPCA and some of the papers got wind of some of the things they were monkeyin' around with and there was a lot of gab back and forth there for a while."

"What happened?"

"Like I say, the government stepped in and put a stop to all the malarky. There was a little last-ditch fight from the churches, I think. But they finally came to realize that this trick was something you couldn't stop. It couldn't be called evil any more than fire or electricity or atomic power could be called evil, even if they kill a lot of people."

"I see."

"So, as I say, that's about all there was to it. Six months after Congress passed the law forbidding capital punishment, they started the public hatings. It's worked just fine."

"Is this an unusually large crowd?"

"Not for a political prisoner. Some regular old rapists, murderers, some of them don't pull maybe more than twenty, thirty thousand. The people just don't get stirred up enough. They just don't have enough hate in them and if you ain't got enough of that, man, you might as well stay home."

"I suppose so," said Traub.

The sun had come out from behind a cloud now and Traub watched silently as large map-shaped shadows moved majestically across the grass.

"She's warming up," someone said.

"That's right," a voice agreed. "Gonna be real nice."

Traub leaned forward and lowered his head as he retied the laces on his right shoe, and in the next instant he was shocked to attention by a guttural, maniacal roar that was loosed from the crowd's throat. The floor beneath his feet vibrated at the sound as his head snapped up. He looked at the field.

At the far end, in distant right-center field, three men were walking toward the platform. Two were walking together, the third was slouched in front of them, head down, his gait unsteady.

184

Traub had thought he was going to be all right, but now, looking at the tired figure being prodded toward second base, looking at the bare, bald head, he began to feel slightly sick to his stomach.

It seemed to take forever, but at last the three tiny figures reached the platform and the two guards jostled the prisoner up the stairs and toward the small kitchen chair.

When he reached it and seated himself the crowd shouted with renewed vigor. Then a tall, distinguished man stepped to the speaker's lectern and cleared his throat, raising his right hand in an appeal for quiet.

"All right," he said, "all right."

The mob slowly fell silent. Traub clasped his hands tightly together. He felt slighty ashamed.

"All right," said the speaker. "Good afternoon, ladies and gentlemen. On behalf of the President of the United States, I welcome you to another Public Hating. This particular affair," he said, "as you know, is directed against the man who was yesterday judged guilty in United States District Court here in New York City, Professor Arthur Ketteridge."

At the mention of Ketteridge's name the crowd made a noise like an earthquake-rumble. Several pop bottles were thrown, futilely, from the center-field bleachers. They landed nowhere near the platform.

"We will begin in just a moment," said the speaker, "but first I should like to introduce the Reverend Charles Fuller, of the Park Avenue Reformed Church, who will make the invocation."

A small man with glasses stepped forward, replaced the first speaker at the microphone, closed his eyes, and threw back his head.

"Our Heavenly Father," he said, "to whom we are indebted for all the blessings of this life, grant, we beseech Thee, that we act today in justice and in the spirit of truth. Grant, O Lord, we pray Thee, that what we are about to do here today will render us the humble servants of Thy divine will. For it is written: *the wages of sin is death*. Have pity on this wayward soul who is about to be committed back into Thy personal care, O Lord. Search deep into his heart for the seed of repentance, if there be such, and if there be not, plant it therein, O Lord, in Thy goodness and mercy."

There was a slight pause. The Reverend Fuller coughed and then said, "Amen."

The crowd, which had stood quietly during the prayer, now seated itself and began to buzz again.

Traub nudged his companion.

"Tell me," he said, "do these things ever misfire?"

"Not that I ever heard of," said the other. "Why?"

"Oh, no particular reason," said Traub. "I was just wondering."

"No, this hatred is a pretty effective thing," said the man, lighting a cigar. "Like I said before, it's a wonder it took such a damned long time before they figured it out."

"I guess it is."

"They started it, I think, kicking around the old story about people dying of broken hearts and that sort of

186

thing. Folks just wasting away when they lost loved ones. That kind of stuff. Then somebody combined it with these experiments with the rats and monkeys and there you were."

"The power of rejection is something, all right," agreed Traub. "I guess this thing is rooted in Freud, too, eh?"

"Freud, Schmeud," said the man. "It don't take no big-dome to tell you that a kid breaks up if his mother kicks him out or gives him a rough time. You take away love and anybody will be hurt, but you replace affection with some nice, powerful hatred and brother, you've had it!"

"Reminiscent of voodoo," said Traub.

"Guess it is," said the other.

"But you know," said Traub, "it just occurred to me; it isn't the mechanical plausibility of the thing that frightens me. It's the public spectacle of it that——"

"Better cut that kind of talk," said the man. "What do you want people to do? Mail in their hatred? You gotta *be* there. You gotta be right on the scene. You gotta keep whipped up. And what the hell's so unusual about a public execution? For thousands of years that's about the only kind there were. Burning at the stake, lynching, the firing squad. Hell, even after they started with the electric chair and the gas chamber you could still see the damned thing if you wanted to, like if you were a newspaperman or something. This passion for privacy at executions is a pretty new idea and as far as I'm concerned it was started by either a bunch of pantywaists or by guys who were afraid they were killing innocent men."

On the platform the speaker was again addressing the crowd.

"All right," he said. "You know why you were invited here today. You know that we all have a job to do. And you know why we have to do it."

"Yes!" screamed thousands of voices.

"Then let us get to the business at hand. At this time I would like to introduce to you a very great American who, to use the old phrase, needs no introduction. Former President of Harvard University, current adviser to the Secretary of State, ladies and gentlemen, here is Dr. Howard S. Weltmer."

A wave of applause vibrated the air in the stadium.

Dr. Weltmer stepped forward, shook hands with the speaker, and adjusted the microphone.

"Thank you," he said. "Now we won't waste any more time here since what we are about to do will take every bit of our energy and concentration if it is to be successfully accomplished. I ask you all," he said, "to direct your unwavering attention toward the man seated in the chair to my left here, a man who in my opinion is the most despicable criminal of our time, Professor Arthur Ketteridge!"

The mob shrieked at this mention of Ketteridge's name. A woman seated near Traub fainted.

"I ask you," said Weltmer, "to rise. That's it, everybody stand up. Now. I want every one of you . . . I understand we have upward of seventy thousand people here today . . . I want every single one of you to stare directly at this fiend in human form, Ketteridge. I want you to let him know by the wondrous power that lies in the strength of your emotional reservoirs, I want you to let him know that he is a criminal, that he is worse than a murderer, that he has committed treason, that he is not loved by anyone, anywhere in the universe, and that he is, rather, despised with a vigor equal in heat to the power of the sun itself!"

People around Traub were shaking their fists now. Their eyes were narrowed; their mouths turned down at the corners.

"Come on," shouted Weltmer. "Let's feel it! Work it out of yourselves. Work out every bit of hatred you've stored up, not only for this man but for anyone. Work it all out, use up all the hatred, the hatred that ordinarily is unproductive, even sinful, but that today has a fine and good purpose. Let us feel it. Let it burn out of your eyes."

Traub was on his feet and under the spell of the speaker he was suddenly horrified to find that his blood was racing, his heart pounding. He felt anger surging up within him. He could not believe that he hated Ketteridge. But he could not deny that he hated something.

"On the souls of your mothers," Weltmer was saying. "On the future of your children, out of your love for your country, I ask you, I demand of you that you release the inhibitions that are damming up some part of your animal power to despise. I want you to become ferocious. I want you to become as the beasts of the jungle, as furious as they in the defense of their homes. They would kill to defend their own. Would you?"

The "yes" that followed took Traub's breath away. It pounded against his ears like the sound of cannon.

Weltmer's voice was getting louder.

"Do you hate this man?" he demanded.

"Yes!" shouted the mob.

"Fiend!" cried Weltmer. "Enemy of the people! Do you *hear*, Ketteridge?"

Traub watched in dry-mouthed fascination as the slumped figure in the chair straightened up convulsively and jerked at his collar. At this first indication that the power of their venom was reaching home, the crowd rose to a new peak of excitement.

"We plead," said Weltmer, "with you people watching today on your television sets, to join with us in hating this wretch. All over America stand up, if you will, in your living rooms. Face the East. Face New York City, if you will, and let anger bubble up in your hearts. Speak it out, let it flow!"

A man beside Traub sat down, turned aside, and vomited softly into a handkerchief, swearing the while. Traub picked up the binoculars the man had discarded for the moment and fastened them fuzzily on Ketteridge's figure, twirling the focus knobs furiously. In a moment the man leaped into the foreground. Traub saw that his eyes were full of tears, that his body was wracked with sobs, that he was in obvious pain.

"He is not fit to live," Weltmer was shouting. "Turn your anger upon him. Channel it. Make it productive.

Be not angry with your family, your friends, your fellow citizens, but let your anger pour out in a violent torrent on the head of this human devil," screamed Weltmer. "Come on! Let's do it! Let's get it over with!"

Traub was in the moment at last convinced of the enormity of Ketteridge's crime and that was when Weltmer said, "All right, that's it. Now let's get down to brass tacks. Let's concentrate on his right arm. Hate it, do you hear. Burn the flesh from the bone! You can do it! Come on! Burn him alive!"

Traub stared unblinking through the binoculars at Ketteridge's right arm as the prisoner leaped to his feet and ripped off his jacket, howling. With his left hand he gripped his right forearm and then Traub saw the flesh turning dark. First a deep red and then a livid purple. The fingers contracted and Ketteridge whirled on his small platform like a dervish, slapping his arm against his side.

"That's it," Weltmer called. "You're doing it. You're doing it. Mind over matter! That's it. Burn this offending flesh. Be as the avenging angels of the lord. Smite this devil! That's it!"

The flesh was turning darker now, across the shoulders, as Ketteridge tore his shirt off. Suddenly, crying out in a loud voice, he broke away from his chair and leaped off the platform, landing on his knees on the grass.

"Oh, the power is wonderful," cried Weltmer. "You've got him. Now let's really turn it on. Come on!"

Ketteridge writhed on the grass and then rose and

began running back and forth, directionless, like a worm on a griddle.

Traub could watch no longer. He put down the binoculars and staggered back up the aisle.

Outside the stadium he walked for twelve blocks before he hailed a cab.